THE INCREDIBLE SHRINKING GHOST

Brian Moses

CANDY JAR BOOKS · CARDIFF
2023

The right of Brian Moses to be identified as the
Author of the Work has been asserted by him in accordance
with the Copyright, Designs and Patents Act 1988.

The Incredible Shrinking Ghost © Brian Moses 2023

Editor: Will Rees
Editorial: Shaun Russell
Cover by Martin Baines

Printed and bound in the UK by
4edge, 22 Eldon Way, Hockley, Essex, SS5 4AD

ISBN: 978-1-915439-70-3

Published by
Candy Jar Books
Mackintosh House
136 Newport Road, Cardiff, CF24 1DJ
www.candyjarbooks.co.uk

For children and staff at
The Churchill School, Hawkinge.

CHAPTER ONE

'Do you think ghosts can kiss each other?'

Alex directed the question at his twin sister, Phoebe, who was sitting beside him in the village churchyard, leaning against a gravestone.

'I mean,' Alex added, 'kissing is pretty gross when you think about it, so I don't know why ghosts would even want to try it. But if they did, how would they manage it?'

The two of them regularly came to the churchyard after school, and quite often they found themselves talking about ghosts. Over the past eleven years, Alex had learnt that Phoebe usually thought a lot before she answered his questions. She was thinking now, he could see that.

Finally, Phoebe replied, 'I really don't know what ghosts would do if they kissed each other. I don't think we'd hear very much. Surely it would be like watching a silent film, with maybe a bit of a hiss when their lips met.'

Phoebe was wondering whether their mum and dad still kissed each other. She didn't see them being

1

affectionate very often. Maybe it was the job they did. Perhaps being in charge of the village funeral parlour made them more serious. The villagers would come to them with all sorts of difficult questions. And Phoebe knew what that was like. She and Alex, as children of undertakers, were always being asked all sorts of gruesome things by other children in the village.

Phoebe always seemed to look pale, as if she'd been hidden away in the dark recesses of the building they lived in, and was only occasionally allowed out into the sunlight. Alex, by contrast, always seemed to have a smile on his face and a mischievous air about him. This led people to think that he'd either just done something he shouldn't, or else was thinking of doing so.

The churchyard was next to the funeral parlour. It was full of ancient yew trees and prickly holly bushes. The gravestone, between two such bushes, was somewhere they liked to sit, and although Phoebe thought it might be a bit disrespectful to perch on somebody's final resting place, it was comfortable to lean back against the stone. Alex never sat still for long. He would soon be up, leapfrogging over the stone, trying to see how many jumps he could complete before he fell down exhausted.

Inscribed on the stone were the words, 'John Taylor, a just and upright man. 1777-1845'. Phoebe and Alex had both remarked that he couldn't be very 'upright' in his present situation.

Alex suddenly jumped up and turned to face Phoebe, struck with a new idea.

'Answer me this. What if you were a headless ghost and you desperately wanted to kiss another headless ghost? Could two floating heads kiss? If only we could meet a ghost, then we could ask one.' Alex paused, considering. 'They might even give us a demonstration.'

Phoebe smiled. 'If you saw a ghost, whether it could kiss or not would be the last thing on your mind. You'd be too busy running away.'

'I'm not sure that I would. I mean, wouldn't you want to interview a ghost if you could? There would be so many things we could find out. Tell you what, let's make a list,' said Alex.

Phoebe searched in her bag for paper and a pen. She knew that Alex wouldn't have either. She was always the practical one.

'First question of mine, Alex began, 'would be can you kiss another ghost?'

Phoebe sighed and wrote it down. 'Do you get wet when it rains?' she added. 'Are you always cold or can you get warm? Do you get blown away in the wind?'

'I've got another one,' said Alex. 'Do ghosts use the toilet?'

'I'm stopping there,' Phoebe said, 'if that's all you can think to ask. Why is it that in any conversation we have, at some point you seem to want to talk about toilets?'

'It's important,' said Alex. 'It's something I really want to know.'

'Well, I've never heard of a ghost eating, have you? And if they don't eat, then I can't imagine that they need to do the other thing either. It's a silly question.'

'Well, what about asking if ghosts can walk through walls? That's something I've always wanted to know. And what about asking a ghost what he really misses about being alive?'

Now that is a good question, Phoebe thought. She added it to the list.

Phoebe and Alex had both tried on a number of occasions to find out what their parents thought about ghosts, but it was a subject that neither of them would discuss. Alex had once had a book of jokes about ghosts, which he and Phoebe found very funny, but whenever he'd tried one out on their parents, there had been very little response. Trying to get them to laugh about anything was really hard work sometimes.

As they thought on, both Phoebe and Alex began to think they could hear whispering coming from the holly bushes behind them.

'It's just the breeze,' Alex said. 'You remember that personification stuff we learnt at school, giving human qualities to something that isn't human? It's just that, just the whisperings of the wind.'

Phoebe wasn't so sure. She thought it sounded more like someone breathing. Then she felt something cold on the back of her neck. She turned and looked at

Alex. He must have put something there.

'Why did you do that?' she asked him.

'Do what? I didn't do anything.'

'You did,' said Phoebe, annoyed at such a blatant lie. 'You put something cold on the back of my neck. Nobody else was near enough to do that. It must have been you.'

'I didn't. It wasn't me, honestly.'

Seconds later, Alex felt something tickle his neck. He shivered.

They both looked around, half expecting to see someone darting between the gravestones. Phoebe moved closer to Alex. It was a chilly day, and even though they were wearing coats, they felt the temperature drop and it suddenly became icy cold. They both shivered. It happened again – cold, then icy cold, then warmer.

'Let's go home,' Phoebe whispered. 'I don't like this. I read somewhere that a sudden drop in temperature is a sign that ghosts are near.'

'Now you're being silly,' said Alex. 'Ghosts can't be seen in the daytime.'

It was then that they heard a third voice, a crackle of a voice, a voice both old and young at the same time. 'Oh, but they can…'

CHAPTER TWO

Phoebe and Alex clutched each other. Who had spoken? Where was the voice coming from?

They looked around but saw no one. Then they looked back at the church.

Sitting on a ledge just above their heads was a small boy, or rather, the shape of a small boy. They could see his outline and tell that his clothes were not any sort they'd seen for sale in shops today. Somehow, they could see light shining through him.

'So, you can see me then?' the boy said.

Alex swallowed hard. 'Yes.' His voice came out as a bit of a croak. 'I can see you. How did you get up there?'

'I can go anywhere I like,' the boy replied.

'But there's no way up there, it's impossible!'

'Not to me,' the boy said. 'Nothing's impossible when you can float.'

'Float? What do you mean?'

'Watch me.'

The boy slowly drifted off the ledge and up into the air. His legs morphed into a ghost-like tail, and he put his arms behind his head and floated. It was like he was floating on water. Then he drifted back to the ledge again and his legs morphed back.

Alex and Phoebe were both stunned. There was no possible explanation. Well, nothing that made any sense, unless...

'Are you a ghost?' Phoebe asked.

'Yes, I am, and a pretty good one too, even if I say so myself.'

'B... b... b... but...' Alex stuttered.

'But I thought ghosts were old, not young children?' Phoebe filled in for him.

'It all depends how old you were when you passed on, doesn't it? I was only ten. I had an accident.'

'What happened to you?'

'I fell off a roof and plunged to the ground. Died instantly.'

'That's awful,' Alex said.

'Well, it wasn't much fun at the time, but it was years ago. Someone called George the First was king. I think a lot of time has passed since then.'

'And so you came back as a ghost?'

'Yes, that's me. Walter the ghost. Sometimes I think it's really good being a ghost, but most of the time I don't. Most of the time it's dead boring, hanging around for years and years, doing nothing except wandering around the churchyard, leapfrogging tombstones.

'Most of the time I'm out and about in the daytime,

just to liven things up a bit. I have fun with the people who visit the churchyard. I follow them around, give them an icy feeling when I pass through them...'

'So that was you,' Phoebe said, 'just now when we were feeling cold.'

'I'm afraid it was, sorry.'

This was crazy, it couldn't be true. Talking to a ghost in broad daylight! Phoebe couldn't believe it.

'But aren't people scared of you?' Alex asked.

'Most of them don't see me – adults that is. Children do, that's the fun bit. Either they're curious and keep trying to point me out to their parents, who can't understand what their kids are getting excited about, or they hide behind their parents and keep sneaking looks at me.'

'So why can children see you and not adults?' asked Alex.

'I don't really know,' Walter replied. 'Can't work it out. I think sometimes that people can only see me when I want them to. So I guess I feel differently about children than I do adults, which must make me more visible.'

'What do you mean by that?'

'Well,' Walter went on, 'I like to play with the children. I pull faces and wink at them. They pull faces back too, and we hold winking contests. Sometimes we play hide and seek. It's a great place, the churchyard, for hide and seek.'

'Yes, I can see that,' said Alex looking round at all

the tangled undergrowth and shadowy corners.

'Sometimes when there's a wedding taking place at the church, I pose for family photographs. I had no idea what they were doing to start with, when they pointed cameras at each other. I learnt what they were called by listening to the adults, and I also found out that these wonderful inventions took pictures, like paintings but more real. I seem to appear in pictures for some reason, I don't know why.

'Sometimes there were cameras that gave you an instant picture, and I'd gaze over the shoulders of the people looking at them. They were always so surprised to find me in their wedding photographs!'

'I suppose they would be,' said Alex. 'But going back to what you said earlier, why did you want us to see you, and why haven't we seen you before?'

'Well, I have been spying on you when you visit, and you seem like the sort of children I would have been friends with when I was alive. Then I heard you talking about ghosts, and it finally seemed like the right moment to show myself. See, I've been trying to find some friends who might be able to help me with something.'

'What sort of help do you need?'

'I want to know whether I can leave this place. You just don't know how bored I've been for the last three hundred years. There's a whole world outside these church gates, and if I'm going to be a ghost forever, I'd like to see some of it. I've been reading the newspapers that blow into the churchyard on windy days, and I've looked at all the pictures. I want to see the sea, to glimpse ocean liners, to fly on a plane… Most of all, I want to go skateboarding. It looks so much fun!

'Besides, there might be another stage to the afterlife, and maybe I'll find it if I can get out of here.'

'Why can't you leave?'

'Believe me, I've tried. I couldn't count how many times I've tried, but there seems to be an invisible wall around the churchyard that's stopping me from leaving. I just can't find a way past it.'

'I've read about something like that,' said Alex. 'It's called a force field, I think.'

'So how can we help you?' said Phoebe.

'Well, I don't know, I'm not sure about this, but I'm thinking that if I can't leave by myself, maybe I can leave if someone takes me with them.'

Phoebe didn't know what to say. Could they really just walk out with a ghost? How would that work? They surely couldn't just stroll out hand in hand? This was getting more and more ridiculous!

'How would we do it?' Alex asked.

'Well, I've learnt over the years that I can shrink in size, just like one of those colourful balloons that children sometimes have. I saw a girl blow up a balloon once and then let it go. It whizzed around the graveyard and shrank in size till it was a tiny thing. I can do that too.'

'Could you shrink small enough to fit in my pocket?' Alex asked.

'I think so. Shall I try?'

'Go on.'

The boy's face twisted as if in pain. He wrapped his arms around himself and squeezed. Nothing happened at first, but after a minute or so had passed, Alex could see that the boy was getting smaller, and smaller, and smaller until he was barely visible. This shrinking was accompanied by what his mum would have called a rude noise, as if someone was attempting to break the world record for the longest ever fart.

A few seconds later, as the noise stopped, Alex felt something wriggling into the pocket of his jeans, and a muffled voice called out, 'Done it!'

'So what do we do now?' Alex managed to ask.

'Let's see if you can walk through the church gate with me in your pocket,' Walter said.

CHAPTER THREE

W*e should be scared,* Alex thought, *but it's hard to be scared with something wriggling around in my pocket, tickling me in places I've never been tickled before.*

Alex found it was impossible to walk sensibly at all. He kept flinging out his legs at strange angles. The wriggling would stop suddenly, then start again, and he found himself jerking around in a peculiar kind of dance. 'Can't you keep still?' he called out to the wriggling bulge in his pocket.

'Sorry,' came the reply. 'I just can't get comfortable.'

Phoebe was finding it all very amusing. It reminded her of the time when her brother thought he could be a world champion breakdancer. With Walter's help he looked as if he might finally succeed.

Alex hadn't seen his sister laugh so much for a long time, if ever. He was so glad that there was nobody else around to witness his strange performance.

Gradually they moved towards the church gate, which was inside an iron archway. Phoebe got there first, unlatched the gate and opened it so that they could pass though. She walked through and waited on the other side while Alex paused just inside the gate.

They heard Walter's voice from Alex's pocket. 'Go on, try it, see if you can do it.'

Alex moved forwards, but slowly, his arms out in front of him in case he should meet something solid. Very soon it began to feel as if he were pushing against air that was forcing him back. There was nothing strange to see – just the gate, his sister, and the street beyond – but all around him it felt like the air was solidifying. He was leaning into it, pushing as hard as he could. He heard Walter's muffled voice, 'Don't stop, keep going, you can do it!'

Alex turned his body and pushed with his shoulder, then turned again and shoved with his other shoulder. He was leaning at the sort of angle where, if this were ordinary air, he'd have fallen straight to the floor. There really was no explanation for this at all.

Finally, just when he thought that he'd exhausted himself, he felt his right arm break free of whatever it was that was holding him. Then the other arm was free, and it seemed as if something had ripped in front of him as he fell to his knees. He kicked backwards with his feet and was finally out in the open.

Walter's voice was full of admiration for what Alex had accomplished. 'You've done it, I'm free!' he yelled gleefully.

From deep inside his trouser pocket, Alex felt Walter wriggling around again, and then the voice answered, 'Well, actually, I'm not free. There's something sticky in here and I appear to be stuck.'

Alex remembered the fudge that had got soft in his pocket a few days ago. It must have left sticky traces and now Walter was having trouble escaping.

'Can I help?' Alex inquired.

'I think it's just a matter of taking it slowly. Bit by bit.'

Alex felt jerky movements inside his pocket as Walter did his best to free himself. 'Trouble is,' Walter spoke as if through gritted teeth, 'every time I free up part of myself, I get caught somewhere else. Trust me to choose someone with a mucky pocket like yours.'

Finally with a huge pull, Walter freed himself and floated from Alex's pocket.

'Look,' Phoebe said, 'we really do have to get home now. You've proven you can break out. Now you can have a think where you would like to visit first. Let's just get you back in for the night, and then we must run.'

Gradually Walter grew in size again. 'You will come and see me again?' he asked, unable to hide his disappointment. 'It's been great having you to talk to. The others are all right but they're not my age. All they do is boss me around.'

'What do you mean, others?' said Phoebe. 'Do you mean there are more ghosts in the churchyard?'

'Of course,' said Walter. 'They're just as desperate to know if they can leave as I was.'

'Well, who are they?' asked Alex. 'Or should I say,

who were they?'

'There's Minnie. She was my teacher. She keeps telling me how useless I am. Then there's Ned. He was the cook in the big house next to the church, the one where I lived. He's been out to get me for the past three hundred years. Most of the time he wanders around with a rolling pin, grunting and growling and calling my name.'

Alex and Phoebe looked at each other. They could both tell what the other was thinking. We don't want to meet Ned!

'Is that everyone?' Alex asked.

'Yes. We're the left behinds, the forsaken ones, condemned to drift for all eternity.'

'Why didn't we see them just now?'

'Most days they can't be bothered to go anywhere. All they do is stay where they are and sleep. I can't do that, I'm too restless. Probably because I'm a young ghost. I still seem to have lots of energy. Minnie and Ned look as if all their energy has been sucked out of them. They're boring.'

Behind them, the church clock struck six o'clock. 'We need to go,' Phoebe insisted. 'We can't stay any longer.'

'Right,' said Walter. 'But you must come and see me again. Please.'

Sorrowfully Walter floated back towards the church gate, waving goodbye to his new friends – but it seemed that whatever it was that had stopped him leaving was now stopping him getting back in. He just floated there, his expression straining as he pushed against the invisible barrier.

'I'll try floating higher,' Walter said.

He did, but it made no difference. 'Perhaps if I shrink again and go back into your pocket, you might be able to get me back inside. I'll try a different pocket this time.'

His face twisted again as he wrapped his arms around himself and slowly shrank in size. They heard the same rude noise as before and Alex felt a wriggle in his pocket.

Alex strode confidently towards the churchyard, but he was met with an invisible wall. Try as he might, he just couldn't pass through. If the first time round, on their way out, the barrier had felt like wading through particularly sticky custard, it now felt like solid rock.

He tried again and again, but finally he had to admit defeat.

'What do we do now?' he asked Phoebe.

Phoebe usually had an answer to everything, but on this occasion she was stumped. She was desperate to start heading for home as they were already late for tea.

'Do you actually want to go back into the churchyard?' Alex asked. 'You could start to do all those things you want to do, go off on your travels, see the world…'

Walter spoke softly, 'Now that I'm out, I'm a little bit scared. Can I stay with you two for a while and get used to things?'

Phoebe was thinking again. Alex knew when she was deep in thought by the way her forehead crinkled as she concentrated. He waited to see if she came up with anything. Finally, she spoke.

'We should take Walter home with us for the night, keep him hidden, and tomorrow after school, we'll come back here and try to find some way of getting him back where he belongs. That seems to me to be the only solution.'

'But how can I go home with a ghost in my pocket?' Alex protested. 'Something's bound to go wrong somewhere.'

'I can't see any alternative, can you?'

'Hey, wait a minute,' Walter's muffled voice said from Alex's pocket. 'Don't you think you should ask my opinion before you decide my future?'

'We're sorry, Walter,' said Phoebe, thinking how ridiculous this evening had become. Not only had their whole thinking about ghosts been turned upside down, now she found herself apologising to one!

'Well, what's your solution then?'

Walter's voice was soft and edged with worry. 'I don't know. I just don't know what's going to happen to me. I never expected to find that I couldn't get back into the churchyard. It never crossed my mind.'

'Right,' said Phoebe decisively. She knew what her mum would advise, and it was the most sensible advice there was. 'This is what's going to happen. We're going to sleep on it. You'll go home with us for the night, and then hopefully we'll sort it all out tomorrow.'

CHAPTER FOUR

Alex and Phoebe entered their house through the back. As quietly as he could, Alex closed the door, tiptoed through the kitchen and along the hall to the stairs. Fortunately, both their parents were in the lounge watching the *Six O'clock News*. The twins couldn't understand why they insisted on watching the news every night. It only ever seemed to upset them. Phoebe went in to see them while Alex carefully climbed the stairs, avoiding the fifth stair that always creaked. His room was the first door that he came to, and in a moment he had dashed through and closed the door tightly behind.

'You can come out now,' he whispered to Walter.

Walter sat himself on the top shelf of the bookcase and slowly grew in size until he was about the size of a rabbit.

'Well, that was some effort,' he said. 'In fact, this escape from the churchyard has really tired me out. I thought I wouldn't be able to sleep with all the excitement, but I warn you, I don't think I'll be good for anything till I've had a long sleep.'

In some ways Alex was disappointed. There was so much that he wanted to ask Walter and so much he wanted to do with him. The thought of him being inactive for a while was a real letdown. However, he supposed at least it would be easier to keep him hidden while he and Phoebe came up with a plan.

'Where will you sleep?' asked Alex.

'I think I could probably make myself comfortable on top of your bookcase. Have you, by any chance, got something soft that I could lie on?'

Alex pulled out a couple of scarves from a drawer, folded them, and standing on a chair, managed to spread them out along the shelf. By the time he was finished, it looked quite cosy.

Walter lay down on the scarves, wriggling himself into comfy position. 'This,' he said with satisfaction, 'should do very well.'

With that he yawned again, closed his eyes, and as far as Alex could tell, fell fast asleep.

Once Phoebe had come upstairs, Alex showed her where Walter was sleeping.

'This is so weird,' she said, 'but it's exciting too. Do you think anyone else has ever found themselves a pet ghost?'

'I doubt it,' Alex said. 'But I'm worried we've just found ourselves a huge heap of trouble.'

Later that evening, when Alex turned off his bedside light, he knew there was no way he'd get to sleep.

His head was spinning. Last night he wouldn't have believed that there were such things as ghosts, but now, he couldn't not believe. The evidence was there before his eyes, in his room, sleeping soundly, while he lay awake and restless. The questions went round and round in his mind. Who could he tell? Would anyone believe him if he did?

Alex tossed and turned but sleep just wouldn't come. Moments later he heard a noise, a rumbling sound that, if he wasn't mistaken, sounded like somebody snoring. Probably Dad, he thought. Usually Mum would give him a quick dig in the ribs to shut him up, but on this occasion the sound went on. Not only that, it was increasing in volume. What could it be?

Before he could investigate, his light went on and the door was pushed open.

'Alex,' his mum called, 'is that you making that noise? Whatever are you up to? You woke me up!'

'It's not me!' Alex protested.

'Well, who is it then? It's not Phoebe and I hardly think there's anyone else sleeping in your room.'

Alex realised that the noise had stopped, and he realised it must have been Walter. But how could he explain it away to his mum? There was no way he could tell her the truth. She'd never believe him!

'Well you shouldn't be snoring at your age,' Mum said. 'Turn over on your side and go back to sleep. I'll see you in the morning.'

Switching the light off behind her, she pulled the door to, and Alex listened as she padded across the landing and back to bed.

Quietly, Alex got out of bed and tiptoed over to the bookshelves.

'That was you, Walter, wasn't it?' he whispered.

'I think it probably was,' Walter replied. 'I'm very sorry. I think my nose must be blocked with dust from that churchyard. There's some very dusty corners in that old place.'

'I can't have you doing that again,' Alex said. 'I think you'd better move into my wardrobe. That should muffle any sounds that you make.'

Walter was still no bigger than a rabbit. He floated down from the shelf while Alex spread some sweatshirts at the base of the cupboard. He helped Walter climb in and watched while Walter wriggled around, trying to get comfortable.

'If you've got to snore,' he warned Walter, 'snore quietly.' And with that, he closed the wardrobe door.

Alex lay awake for a long time. He heard brief bouts of snoring now and then, but fortunately none were loud enough to trouble Alex's mother.

Eventually he drifted off to sleep. Usually, he dreamt some very odd dreams – sometimes he wondered just where they came from – but there was nothing in his dreams that night that matched the day he'd just had.

CHAPTER FIVE

'You must have seen a dead body. Your parents are undertakers! Come on, admit it.'

It was next morning, just before school started, and Rafe, one of the boys in their class, was off on his favourite subject again. His question was addressed, as always, to Phoebe and Alex.

'You can't deny,' Rafe continued, 'that they bring the dead 'uns to your place to measure them up for a coffin. You must have seen one.'

'We don't see anything,' Phoebe said. 'It all happens in the offices at the back. Our part of the house is at the front, and it's separate from the rest of the building. So why don't you stop going on and on about it? We haven't seen one and we won't ever. That's final.'

Phoebe hated being the centre of attention. She'd had to get used to it though. She was the brains of the class, the one everyone turned to when they had a problem to be solved.

Rafe, on the other hand, was a farmer's son. He'd been present at the birth and death of farm animals, and liked to boast that nothing bothered him. He wasn't one of Alex's mates, and Alex was wary of annoying him, although he hated to see Phoebe picked on.

But Rafe wasn't about to let it rest. He started up on Phoebe again. 'You'd be too scared, I bet that's it. I bet you could see one if you wanted to.'

Phoebe gave him a withering look. 'You're just mouthing off. You wouldn't see it through, even if the opportunity was there for you. There's no way you'd lift a coffin lid and look inside.'

'Oh yes I would. I'd do it straightaway. A conversation with a corpse, that would be brilliant. I'd take a selfie with it too.'

Alex couldn't help thinking that it would be a short and somewhat one-sided conversation, but he kept that thought to himself.

Rafe kept on at Phoebe. 'Look, can't you invite me round one day after school. You can keep your parents talking somewhere while I sneak into wherever it is they keep the bodies and take a peep. That shouldn't be too difficult.'

Phoebe's friends, Fleur and Alice, were pulling her arm, trying to get her to move away from Rafe, but she was determined to have the last word.

'Rafe, is there any way of getting this into that thick skull of yours? There's *no way* that it will ever happen. You are never going to be invited back for tea at my place, and you are never, repeat never, lifting the lid on one of our coffins. It's disrespectful for a start. The dead are dead, they're not there to be gawped at by sensation seekers like you. Just forget it and stop pestering me.'

'You'll change your mind,' Rafe said. 'I'd bet on it.'

Watching this familiar scene, Alex wondered about Rafe. He had seen his parents on a couple of occasions, waiting for Rafe after school, or dragging him around one of the village shops on the weekend. They never seemed that interested in their son and seldom turned up for parents' evenings. Phoebe had used to feel sorry for him, but then she'd heard about the ways that Rafe was sometimes unkind to the animals on the farm. She hated to think about that.

Alex wondered, too, about Rafe's fascination with everything that most people tried not to think about. It had started in Year 3, when every story he'd written featured zombies. His teacher finally declared class 3 to be a 'zombie free zone' and banned him from writing about them. Then in Year 4, he'd loved finding out all the gruesome facts about mummification when they'd studied the Egyptians, while in Year 5 he'd taken great pleasure in finding out all the most horrible details of Tudor executions.

Rafe never seemed content to keep his gruesome knowledge to himself and was forever calling out in class to reveal his latest grisly discovery. He always volunteered to narrate the ghost stories when they were assigned books to read in class. Wanting to come face-to-face with a real dead body was just a natural progression for Rafe and his bizarre fascinations.

But Alex knew something Rafe didn't. He knew that he and his sister were in possession of a hugely powerful secret. They'd discovered that ghosts existed. Not only that, but one was at their home right now, fast asleep in Alex's wardrobe.

Mondays were tidying up days for Mrs Mitchell, and there was usually a lot of tidying to do after a busy weekend. She spent the morning cleaning the bathroom and hoovering the bedrooms, and now there was just Alex's room left to clean.

While she was dusting, she found a couple of scarves on top of Alex's bookshelves and wondered what they were doing there. She put them away in a drawer and then wheeled in the vacuum cleaner.

Inside the wardrobe, although deep in his slumbers, Walter heard a sound. Slowly he woke up and lay in the dark, listening. It took a moment for him to remember where he was. He heard someone moving around the room and then a sound like a dragon's roar. He pressed his hands against his ears. He had seen vacuum cleaners in action before, when he'd explored the church, and had come to the conclusion that they were designed to clean the place. In the church, however, he'd always been able to move away from them and find somewhere quieter until they went away again.

This time, though, there was no escape, and the

noise went on and on till suddenly the wardrobe door was pulled open, and it got louder still. Walter wasn't too worried. He knew that he couldn't be seen. But as Alex's mum brandished a long tube, pointing it in his direction, he realised he was in trouble.

She reached in and picked up the sweatshirts that Alex had laid out for Walter to lie on, toppling him onto the floor of the wardrobe. Then she pulled out several pairs of Alex's shoes. Walter dodged a pair of sweaty trainers, then some mud-encrusted boots, and decided that his best bet was to squeeze himself into a corner and shrink down as small as possible. But just as he made his move, he felt himself dragged irresistibly back, unable to resist the pull of the vacuum cleaner.

Walter remembered how strong the wind had felt sometimes when he was alive, how it had pushed against him, tearing at his clothes and snatching at his breath as he struggled to walk into it. Now he felt the same sort of wind pulling him back.

As a ghost, he was very lightweight, and although he clung desperately to whatever, he couldn't help himself from being sucked up into darkness and dust...

CHAPTER SIX

A lex and Phoebe found themselves drifting together throughout the school day, and every time they couldn't help grinning. They shared the most amazing secret. The two of them, alone in all the world, knew something that no one else did. It wasn't something they could talk about, however, unless absolutely alone. All day they were burning to talk to each other about it, but there was no opportunity until afternoon break.

Their class teacher, Mr Khan, was on playground duty. Both Alex and Phoebe really liked their teacher. He was always willing to talk through problems, he knew how to be strict when it was necessary, but he also enjoyed relaxing with his class and telling a joke or two. Spotting Mr Khan across the playground, Alex indicated to Phoebe that he wanted to ask him a question, and marched over, Phoebe close behind him.

'Do you think ghosts exist, Mr Khan?'

Their teacher paused before replying, and when he did it was with another question. 'Why are you asking me that, Alex?'

'No reason really, except that I've been reading a

ghost book and it made me think. So what do you believe, Mr Khan?'

'Well, it's not something I've given a lot of thought to.'

'Well,' Alex persisted, 'have you ever seen one?'

Mr Khan took a sip from the coffee cup that he was holding, then looked round to see if anyone else was nearby before speaking.

'Actually,' he said, 'I did have an experience once. One I've never been able to explain.'

He kept his voice low, as if he was thinking that he probably shouldn't be sharing this story.

'My family and I were staying in a castle. We were on holiday in one of these unusual buildings that some holiday companies rent out to the public. It was fabulous by day, but at night it was a little spooky and we all got a bit jittery. Our two young girls, in particular, felt very nervous.'

'Did you see something?' Alex butted in.

'Well, it was more a case of hearing something. It must have been the third or fourth night we were there, and the four of us had gathered round the kitchen table for our evening meal. Suddenly we heard footsteps coming from the room above. They criss-crossed the room for a minute or so and then they stopped. By this time, of course, we'd worked out that if we were all in the kitchen, then it must be somebody else. We never did find out who. Maybe it was a ghost with heavy boots on. Anyway, the girls were so scared that we all slept downstairs that night.'

'Did it make you believe in ghosts?' Phoebe asked.

'Let's say it made me more open-minded than I had been before. Previously I thought all talk of ghosts was ridiculous, but since then, I'm not so sure.'

'Have you ever heard of any ghosts in the village churchyard?'

'I did actually do a bit of research once, looking at the gravestones, and I did read about a phantom figure that was supposedly seen in the woods. There's also a tale about a ghostly coach and horses. Apparently several people have reported seeing it rattling towards them before it vanishes. I'll try and find out something about it if you're interested.'

'Thanks, Mr Khan, we definitely *are* interested.'

'Well, it's nice to know I'm not alone in that. But now, I'm late blowing the whistle for the end of play.'

Alex and Phoebe were both very pleased when school finished for the afternoon. They were both desperate to see Walter again. There were so many questions they wanted to ask him, and a huge problem that still needed solving: how could they get him back into the churchyard? Would there still be a barrier if they tried again that evening?

They tried to sneak into the house and up to Alex's room without their mum seeing them, but it wasn't to be. She insisted that they sat down with a drink and one of the cupcakes that she'd baked that afternoon. Then she started asking them about what they'd done at school.

Their dog, Sherlock, a fox red Labrador, decided that it would be worth hanging around in case either of them dropped any crumbs onto the floor. He was giving them 'the Labrador look', which they always found hard to resist. They both managed to sneak him something while their mum was looking elsewhere. Finally, they managed to get away by saying they had some homework to complete.

Upstairs in Alex's room, Phoebe closed the door, while Alex eased open the wardrobe.

'They're gone!' he shouted. 'All the sweatshirts I laid down for Walter to lie on, they're not there, and I can't see him anywhere.'

Phoebe and Alex looked at each other in dismay.

'He can't have gone far,' Phoebe said. 'Let's look for him.'

They shifted stuff around in the wardrobe, pulled out shoes and peered inside them, checked the pockets of trousers and coats, but Walter wasn't anywhere to be found. They called his name, looked under the bed, scanned the windowsills and shelves... but he'd disappeared.

'OK. Let's think for a minute. Where might he have gone?' said Phoebe.

'Well, if I wake up in the night, I usually go to the bathroom.'

Phoebe shot him a look, and he remembered their conversation in the churchyard, before Walter had first made his appearance.

'But Walter doesn't eat,' Alex continued quickly, 'so he wouldn't need to do the other thing.'

'Wait a minute,' Phoebe said. 'It's Monday, isn't it? That's the day Mum cleans everywhere. She must have disturbed him.' She broke off suddenly. She'd had a terrible thought.

Alex voiced it for her. 'Mum vacuums our rooms when she cleans… Sheeeesh, I bet that's what happened. Walter must have been asleep and got sucked up by the vacuum cleaner.'

Alex raced downstairs with Phoebe close behind him. They skidded through the kitchen, much to their mum's surprise, and into the utility room.

Mrs Mitchell followed them. She couldn't understand why they were both kneeling down and showing so much interest in her vacuum cleaner.

'Did you vacuum my room today?' Alex asked.

'Yes, I do it every Monday as you know. Why? What's the problem?'

'I've lost something and I'm worried it may have been sucked up into the machine. How do I empty it?'

Just as he asked that question, Alex glimpsed a movement out of the corner of his eye. He turned to focus more clearly on what he was seeing, and there was Walter waving to him from the top of the washing machine.

'Actually it's OK, Mum,' he said. 'I think I've just remembered where I put it.'

Mrs Mitchell knew better than to ask questions. Her

son had always been one for sudden, inexplicable enthusiasms, only to lose interest a minute or two later.

'I'm so glad,' she replied. 'I really don't want you trying to empty that and making a mess everywhere.'

She went back to the kitchen while Alex moved nearer the washing machine. There was a noise like a balloon deflating, and Alex felt something wriggle in his pocket. He nodded at Phoebe and they both headed back to Alex's room.

'How did you escape?' Alex asked Walter, when he had climbed out of Alex's pocket.

'It was a real struggle,' Walter replied. 'I was whirling around with all the dust and dog hairs, desperately trying to find something to cling on to, till suddenly it stopped. Everything went quiet. Then I was being shaken from side to side.'

'That must have been our mum carrying the vacuum cleaner downstairs,' Alex explained.

Walter continued, 'Once it had been quiet and still for a while, I decided to try and escape. I remembered how, if I concentrated hard enough, I was able to travel through walls. So I tried the same thing, and with a bit of extra effort, I found myself emerging from my prison. It wasn't easy though. I was so tired that I lay down and fell asleep. Then you found me.'

Phoebe was looking puzzled. 'If you can travel through walls and escape through the side of a vacuum cleaner, why can't you get through the walls surrounding the churchyard?'

'I just don't know, it's puzzling me too,' said Walter. 'Shall we try again?'

Phoebe looked out the window. It was raining hard outside, and she doubted whether she and Alex would be given permission to go out unless it stopped. 'We may have to wait till tomorrow,' she said.

'Can I ask you a question, Walter?' said Alex.

'Of course you can.'

Alex glanced at Phoebe, then said, 'What's it like – dying, I mean?'

His sister flashed him a look of disapproval as though this was a question he shouldn't be asking.

'Actually, I only had a few seconds to think about it. One minute I was on the roof and next I was plunging to the ground. Then everything went black, although it quickly changed to grey and then white, and I found myself floating above my body and looking down on myself.'

'Were you in pain?' Phoebe asked.

'I wasn't. That was the amazing thing. The body I'd left behind was crumpled up, and there must have been a moment of pain as I hit the ground, but in my ghostly form I felt nothing.'

Phoebe shivered. 'But why were you on the roof?'

'We got into terrible trouble with Ned once. You remember I told you that he was our cook? My friend Rufus and I used to fill our pockets with pebbles and climb through a window onto the roof. We would make our way over the roof until we reached the kitchen, where there was a skylight that could be opened. Below us would be a table with all kinds of pies and dishes full of food. We had such fun dropping pebbles! They'd land – *splat!* – and sink into the food, and no one would notice until the dishes reached the table. Only, one time it was a meal for some very important dinner guests, and they were not very impressed when they found pebbles on their plates.

'My father gave me such a thrashing I couldn't sit down for a week. It didn't stop us, though, and we did it all again a week or so later. And that was when Ned chased us all around the house brandishing his rolling pin. He was threatening us with all kinds of horrible things. Rufus managed to hide, but I couldn't get away, and my only escape was through one of the upstairs windows and out onto the roof. Ned was a… shall we say, a stout figure, and there was no way that he should have tried to follow me. I made it onto the roof but was trapped by a chimney stack that I couldn't get past. He thought he'd got me then, but as he moved to grab me, the edge of the roof gave way and we both fell. That's why he's still trying to get his revenge on me three hundred years later.'

Alex and Phoebe looked at each other. Both were thinking how dreadful it must have been to suffer that kind of fate.

Not only that, but what would it be like if they ran into Ned?

CHAPTER SEVEN

The next day at school, before the nine o'clock bell, Phoebe and Alex were already in the classroom. Mr Khan had spotted them on the playground and asked if they could help him sort some books. While the two of them placed the volumes back on the shelves, Alex revealed to Phoebe that Walter was in his pocket. Phoebe put her hand over her mouth to silence a cry.

'You must be mad!' she said. 'What if he's seen by someone?'

'He won't be,' Alex reassured her. 'He knows that he has to keep still and silent. I was just so worried that something else might happen to him, like it did yesterday. And I thought that we could go straight to the churchyard after school and see if we can get him back there.'

'You're talking about me again, I can hear you,' Walter's raspy voice drifted up from Alex's pocket.

'Sssshhh!' They both hissed, looking around to see if Mr Khan had heard anything. Fortunately, he was too busy peering at his computer screen.

At that moment, Rafe burst into the room. He never missed an opportunity to cause maximum commotion, and this morning was no exception. Mr Khan was irritated, they could see.

'Rafe,' he shouted, 'I have to put up with your noise between the hours of 9am and 3.30pm. It is now only 8.55am and I am still due five more minutes' peace. Kindly leave the room.'

'But Mr Khan, I wanted to—'

'LEAVE!'

One of Rafe's problems was that he never knew when to quit. He just always had to push people that little bit further.

'It's not fair, they're in the room already,' he whined, pointing at Alex and Phoebe.

'They are doing something useful, Rafe. You are not. Leave.'

Rafe did as he was told this time, but was back in a flash as soon as the playground whistle was blown.

'I need to tell you something, Mr Khan.'

'It will have to wait until I've called the register.'

Rafe slouched down in his seat as everyone else came into the room and took their places. Once the register was called, Rafe's hand went up.

'Can I tell you what I found out last night?'

Everyone groaned. They knew that it would be something ghastly, some dreadful, strange but true statement that Rafe thought would shock his classmates. Phoebe could see that Mr Khan was thinking the same as everybody else, but he believed in fairness for everyone, and was prepared to listen to whatever Rafe had to say.

'I read it in a book last night. It was a book of horror stories.'

Everyone groaned again.

'I read about a hand of glory. Do you know what that was, Mr Khan?'

'I do, Rafe, and I'm not sure if it's relevant to the maths lesson we are about to begin. But go on.'

Rafe needed no further encouragement. He looked around the room and paused for maximum impact.

'A hand of glory is the left hand of a man who was hanged for murder. Actually it's the mummified left hand, which has to be removed below the wrist at midnight and by the light of a full moon.'

More groans and expressions of disgust from the class. Rafe ignored them and carried on.

'But the very best thing about a hand of glory is that it can open any door. Wouldn't that be amazing? Just think, you'd be able to go anywhere you wanted to. You'd be able to spy on people, and steal stuff, spend all night in the sports centre, go on the rides at Alton Towers when it was shut... Only problem is, where do I find one?'

'I've probably got an old one you could have,' said Mr Khan. 'I saw it in the cupboard last week when I was tidying up.'

The class laughed. They loved his jokes,

particularly when they were at Rafe's expense.

'Alternatively,' Mr Khan continued, 'have you looked in the Argos catalogue?'

Laughter again from the class. Rafe stared daggers at his classmates.

'I bet I find one, one day.' He turned to Phoebe and hissed at her, 'Then I won't have to ask your permission to see a dead body. I'll just use my hand of glory to open your front door and walk in when you're all asleep.'

'In your dreams, Rafe,' said Phoebe. 'No way is that going to happen. You'd never get past our burglar alarm.'

'Who needs a burglar alarm on an undertakers? Who'd want to steal a stiff?'

'That's more than enough,' said Mr Khan, in the sort of voice that he used when joking was over and it was time to start work. 'Open your books, and get on with your maths.'

Rafe couldn't resist a final stab at Phoebe. 'I bet there's a hand of glory in the churchyard, if we knew where to look, maybe in one of those vaults along the back wall.'

Alex heard a cough that sounded suspiciously as if it came from his trouser pocket, then a familiar raspy voice, 'There is,' said Walter, 'I've seen it.'

It was only a whisper, but it was loud enough to make Rafe turn his head.

Had he heard anything? Alex couldn't tell.

*

After half an hour or so of trying to make his maths make some sort of sense, Alex felt Walter wriggling around in his pocket. It was as always a very ticklish feeling, and Alex was having trouble sitting still.

'Will you stop wriggling?' Alex hissed at Walter.

Whether he had heard Alex or not, Walter must have got himself comfortable, as the movement stopped. Alex was just refocusing on his work when an awful smell filled the classroom.

It really was a truly dreadful smell. Think sewage farm mixed with bad eggs mixed with rotten cabbages mixed with… (this has been left blank for you, the reader, to add in whatever smell you think is most terrible). All those and a lot more.

'It must be coming in from outside,' said Mr Khan. 'Close the windows.'

Several children rushed to obey him, but with all the windows closed the smell was much, much worse.

'I bet that was you, Rafe,' somebody called out, in the way that every class tries to pin the blame on someone.

Mr Khan continued, 'If someone has brought a stink bomb into this room, then I shall be extremely angry with them. Everybody, leave your places and step outside through the door at the back.'

Nobody needed telling a second time. There was a mad stampede to the door. Some children were holding their hands over their noses or pretending to faint, while others still cast accusatory looks at Rafe, who unfortunately did have a history of releasing such smells.

Once outside on the school field, Alex moved a short distance away from the others.

'That was you, wasn't it?' he asked Walter.

'I'm afraid it was. A silent one. Impressive, eh? All that moving and jiggling around made me very uncomfortable'

'It must have been an emanation,' whispered Phoebe.

'A what?'

'It's when gas is released, but not by farting.'

Alex looked at his sister incredulously. 'How do you know that?'

'No idea. Something I read somewhere, I assume. It just stuck in my head.'

'That smell was historical,' said Walter happily, 'and I must admit, I'm quite proud of it.'

Alex thought it must be like having the odour of olden days brought back to life. On balance, he decided, he preferred the modern day.

CHAPTER EIGHT

It was the end of school, and Phoebe and Alex were heading towards the churchyard. Phoebe's friends walked with them, and when they reached the churchyard gates, Phoebe realised they had to make up an excuse as to why they were stopping.

'Our dad's meeting us here,' she blurted out.

'He wants to show us something,' Alex added.

Phoebe's friends didn't seem convinced. What was there to see in a gloomy old graveyard? They walked on all the same.

'Hey, Walter,' Alex called. 'Are you awake?'

A very loud yawning noise came from Alex's pocket, and a sleepy voice answered, 'Well, I wasn't, but I am now. Your teacher goes on and on about grammar! He sent me to sleep after a few minutes or so!'

'He's not too bad,' said Phoebe, springing to Mr Khan's defence. 'There are worse, and we've had most of them.'

'I had one once,' said Walter. 'Dreadful bore. Went on and on, trying to teach us Latin. I ask you, what's the point of Latin? No one ever speaks Latin. It was dead and buried long before I was. Now, are you going to try to get me back?'

As they were standing there, a man and his dog walked past them, and through the churchyard gate as easy as you like. 'I suppose we'd better give it a go, but I'm not hopeful,' said Alex. 'Are you ready, Walter?'

'I'm ready,' Walter replied, 'but I'm not hopeful either.'

They moved towards the churchyard gate. Phoebe went first and walked straight through without a problem, but when Alex and Walter tried to follow, the barrier stopped them short again. It was the same invisible wall as before, and for all Alex pushed and barged, leant and leapt, it wouldn't give at all.

Phoebe came back out again, and they both sat down with their backs to the churchyard wall. 'There's got to be a way,' Alex said. 'Do you know of any other ways in, Walter?'

'Well, I used to climb the walls and try to jump down, but each time I launched myself, something forced me back again. I wonder what would happen if we tried tunnelling beneath the wall.'

Alex and Phoebe looked at each other. They were thinking the same thing. How on earth could they possibly dig a tunnel under the churchyard wall without being seen? Let alone actually making a dent in the ground. Sitting on it now, it felt pretty hard beneath them.

'I think that's a non-starter, Walter,' said Phoebe. 'We'd never be able to do it.'

'What if I know someone who might help us?' said Walter.

'Who?'

'Ned. He's a big guy, very strong. He might help, although he's always really bad-tempered with me.'

'Could a ghost actually hold a shovel and dig with it? I thought you said that there wasn't much you could do as a ghost?' Alex asked.

'I don't know the answer to that,' said Walter. 'But I do know that if a ghost really, *really* wants to do something, then it can sometimes be possible.'

'You know, there's a type of ghost that can move things by the power of thought,' Phoebe mused. 'I read about them recently. It's called a poltergeist.'

'Hey, maybe I'm a polterghost,' said Walter. 'I can sometimes move things with my hand, if I try hard enough, and really focus my mind on what I'm trying to do.'

'Well then,' Phoebe replied, 'surely you really want to get back into the churchyard?'

'Well,' hesitated Walter, 'I suppose for a bit... While I get my bearings in the outside world, at least. There's a lot that's changed while I've been away.'

'I think we should try and meet up with Ned,' Alex decided, surprising himself even as he spoke. 'Let's see what he says. We won't know if we don't ask.'

'If that means a midnight trip to the churchyard,

you can count me out,' Phoebe said.

'Actually, it doesn't,' Walter replied. 'Ned is always out and about when the food van comes along. It parks outside the churchyard. Lots of people visit it to buy food, and the smell is just heavenly.'

Phoebe and Alex looked at each other, puzzled, till Phoebe finally twigged what Walter was talking about.

'You mean the fish and chip van, which stops in the village every Friday evening?'

'We can't eat, of course,' said Walter, 'but the smell reminds us of when we could. We stand there for ages, just sniffing it all in.'

Alex thought to himself how awful that must be. He and Phoebe loved fish and chips. All week he looked forward to Friday evening, when they would have them for their tea.

It seemed like Walter was reading his thoughts.

'There is one big advantage though. To not eating, I mean. It means that I don't have to use the toilet. That's a great relief! I mean, all those times when you're a child, your parents keep saying, have you been, have you been today? Been where? To the toilet! And if I hadn't been for two or three days my mother used to mix up some awful potion and make me swallow it. No, all that stuff goes right out the window when you're a ghost.'

Alex shot Phoebe a look of triumph. 'Told you it was a good question! That's one ticked off the list!'

'But what do we do with Walter till Friday night?'

Phoebe said, ignoring him.

'I think we should take turns with him,' said Alex. 'Mum already thinks I've started snoring. He's stayed in my room for two nights, so you can have him with you tonight. We'll swap back tomorrow.'

'Don't I get a say in all this?' pleaded Walter.

'No!'

CHAPTER NINE

When Phoebe saw Alex at breakfast next morning, she told him that it had been a quiet night. Walter had slept inside her wardrobe and only woken her once with his snoring. Fortunately, her room wasn't so close to their parents' room, so his snores hadn't disturbed them.

'So where is he?' Alex asked.

Phoebe pulled her pencil case out of her bag. 'He's in here.'

That meant another day in school with Walter, hoping and praying that he'd keep quiet. After the mishap with the vacuum cleaner, however, they'd both decided it was better to have Walter with them than risking losing him down a plughole, or up the chimney, or wherever else he might find himself whisked off to. They were Walter's only living friends in the world, and it was their responsibility to look after him.

The day started well. Walter was still sleepy, and apart from a snuffle or two, which Phoebe disguised with a cough, he stayed silent. She left her pencil case on her table at break time but returned to find Rafe standing over it, looking puzzled.

'Have you got something in that pencil case?' he asked her. 'I swear I saw it move.'

Phoebe was horrified, although she tried to keep herself calm.

'Of course I've got something in that pencil case, Rafe,' she said. 'Pencils and pens, like most people have.'

'No, no, no, there's something more than that. It moved, I tell you. Open it up.'

'I will not.'

'I'll open it up then.'

'You won't.'

'Give it to me.'

Rafe made a lunge for Phoebe's pencil case, but she pulled it away from his reach. However, at that moment, Frank, one of Rafe's few friends, appeared behind her and snatched the pencil case out of her hands and ran across the room with it. 'Here, Rafe,' he called out as he lobbed it to him.

Phoebe ran towards Rafe, but he threw it back, over her head, to Frank. Things were just developing into a full blown game of Piggy in the Middle when Mr Khan walked in.

'OK, stop the noise, everyone in their own places now,' he barked out.

From the tone of his teacher's voice, even Rafe knew better than to argue.

'Rafe's got my pencil case, sir!' Phoebe called out.

Mr Khan didn't bother with any investigations. He knew that ninety-nine percent of the time, Rafe was in the wrong. 'Give it back, Rafe – *now*.'

Rafe walked across and placed the pencil case on Phoebe's table. He smiled at her, although she knew that any smile from Rafe was never sincere. He'd be back later, she knew that, and she'd have to take very good care that she didn't leave the pencil case anywhere he could find it.

As she arranged her exercise books on her desk, she heard a groan from inside the case. She needed to look and see what was wrong. She took a gamble.

'Please, Mr Khan, I needed to give the school secretary a message and I forgot. Can I do it quickly, please?'

If it were anyone other than Phoebe, the request would more than likely have been turned down, but in Mr Khan's eyes, Phoebe was totally trustworthy. She knew that too, and felt bad about deceiving him, but it had to be done.

Once outside the classroom she headed for the girls' toilets, where she unzipped the pencil case and discovered Walter curled up in a tiny ball in one of the corners.

'All that tossing and turning made me feel terrible,' he groaned. 'What was going on?'

'Sorry, Walter, it was this stupid boy in our class, but it's over now. He won't get hold of you again.'

'I shrunk myself very, very small and squeezed inside one of your pen lids. I couldn't think of anything else to do. He may not have seen me if he'd looked inside, but I couldn't take that risk. I think I just need to lie down now and recover.'

'I know what I'll do,' Phoebe said. 'I'll put the pencil case in the inside pocket of my coat. It's hanging up in the cloakroom. You shouldn't be disturbed there. It'll be nice and quiet for you.'

The day ran its course. Some of the work was fun, as it often was with Mr Khan, but then he gave out some old SATs test papers, and it stopped being fun very quickly. It wasn't yet time for the tests, but every so often they looked at a practice paper and went through it question by question. Today was one of those days. Phoebe had to borrow a pen and pencil from Alex, and at the end of the day, she wasn't the only member of the class who was glad to be going home.

She fetched her coat from the cloakroom, but from its weight, it was immediately obvious that the pencil case wasn't there. She looked all around, in case it had fallen out, but there was no sign of it anywhere.

She raced out to tell Alex, but he knew already. Rafe was standing at a distance, waving the case in the air. Beside him was his younger sister Fiona. It was obvious that he'd guessed where she'd put the pencil case and sent his sister to steal it.

'Why don't we walk home together and discuss this

little problem that seems to have arisen?' he called out.

'We have nothing to discuss with you, Rafe,' Alex replied. 'Give it back.'

'All in good time. You see, I'd like to strike up a little bargain with you, Phoebe. I'll give it back if you arrange for me to call round to your place and lift a coffin lid. Just a little bit, just so I can take a peep.'

'No way.'

'I think you will,' said Rafe. 'I think there's something in this pencil case that you want very much. I'm not sure what it is yet, but I'm going to find out. So let's leave and walk home all friendly like, so we can discuss how to settle this.'

They left the school and headed towards the churchyard. If you had to pick a word to sum up the expressions on Alex and Phoebe's faces, it would certainly be dismay. They refused to walk alongside Rafe, but hung back, muttering to each other. There was no chance of grabbing the pencil case, though, as Rafe's friend Frank was walking behind him, ready to repel any such challenge. Both of them were bigger and much stronger than Alex, and he knew he wouldn't stand a chance in a fight.

It was starting to seem like the only way to rescue Walter was to agree to Rafe's demands and then think of a way of stopping him later. Shortly, they reached the churchyard gate, and their whispered planning had to stop.

'Why don't we go in and sit somewhere quiet, so that we can work this out?' said Rafe.

He turned to go through the gate but found his progress blocked. He twisted and pushed but there was no way through. It seemed like Rafe would be no more successful than Alex had been, not while he was holding the pencil case with Walter inside it.

Rafe was used to getting his own way, and he got increasingly flustered, struggling against this unseen obstacle. He couldn't understand what was happening. Something was stopping him, invisible yet quite solid.

'What on earth's happening?' he spluttered. 'I can't get through.'

Alex looked at Phoebe. Both knew that, however much Rafe pushed and shoved, it would make no difference. They couldn't help it. They began to giggle.

'You try, Frank,' Phoebe needled. 'See if you can get through.'

Frank walked straight through without trouble, and that just infuriated Rafe even more. Frank strolled back out again and shrugged.

'Push me, Frank,' said Rafe, 'see if that works.'

Frank pushed and pushed but nothing happened. He turned around to lean against Rafe's back and pushed again, but there was still no way through.

Suddenly Rafe's eyes lit up. 'Here, Frank,' he said, passing him the pencil case. 'Let me try again.

And this time, of course, he passed straight through the gate.

'Now you try again, Frank.'

Within a few steps Frank, with the pencil case in his hand, was stopped short. There was no way he could get through.

'I'm beginning to think,' said Rafe, 'that this has something to do with your pencil case, Phoebe. That's why you've been so keen to get hold of it. I think we'll just take a look inside…'

It was all Phoebe could do to stop herself screaming out as she watched Rafe unzip the case and empty the contents onto the pavement. One by one he picked up the items, peering at them, shaking them, then discarding them again. There was nothing unusual to be seen. Rafe just couldn't understand. 'Try walking through with the empty case, Frank.'

Again Frank met an invisible wall. Rafe took the pencil case out of Frank's grip and upended it again, shaking it as hard as he could.

Alex and Phoebe held their breath. They'd both seen it, something the size and shape of a small bubble, floating out of the case and to the ground. It must have taken a supreme effort for Walter to shrink himself to that size. It seemed that Rafe, though, hadn't noticed anything. He was busy peering inside the case and running his finger around the edges. He shook it again. 'There's got to be something here…'

Case in hand, he again tried walking into the churchyard. This time, of course, he got through.

He turned threateningly towards Alex and Phoebe.

'I don't know what you two are up to, and I don't know what's happening here, but nobody, I repeat, *nobody*, makes a monkey out of me.'

Alex couldn't help thinking that ape or gorilla would have been better comparisons, but in the circumstances he kept quiet.

Rafe bent down, picked up Phoebe's pens and pencils and replaced them in the pencil case. 'I'm taking this home,' he said, 'for further investigation. Come on, Frank, let's go.'

CHAPTER TEN

It was turning out to be a difficult week for Phoebe and Alex. Walter was discovering lots of fun new things about the modern world, but with every new fascination, there came fresh worry that their parents would discover him. Then again, it was pretty cool sharing all these new things with him. He looked so funny with Alex's headphones on, listening to the music from Alex's phone. There were several songs that he liked a lot, and while the music played he'd bob up and down in time to the beat. He particularly enjoyed AC/DC's 'Highway to Hell'. Alex had to explain what a highway was, as Walter was worried it had something to do with the highwaymen who'd been out robbing people when he was alive. He also liked Guns 'n' Roses and Black Sabbath, both of which got him fist pumping the air. After they'd shown him the groups performing on YouTube, Alex taught him how to play air guitar, and he floated around the room playing along with every heavy rock song they could find.

On Walter's next night in Phoebe's room, he found

it hard to sleep. The lyrics to the songs Alex had played him kept running through his head. What a wonderful racket! He couldn't sleep after that! He wanted to get up and dance.

'Be quiet, Walter,' Phoebe hissed for the seventh or eighth time that night. 'Go to sleep.'

'I can't, I'm bored. I need to do something. Can I wander about for a bit?'

'Just don't make a noise.'

Although she was worried about what Walter would get up to once he left her room, Phoebe reassured herself that it was late and her parents were already asleep. No one would spot him headbanging, or whatever it was he was planning. She dropped off to sleep pretty quickly.

The next thing she knew, it was morning. She was reassured when she heard small snoring noises coming from Walter, still asleep in her wardrobe. *Nothing much can have happened*, she thought to herself, *nothing that disturbed anyone anyway*.

She left Walter where he was, knocked on Alex's door to wake him, and then went downstairs for breakfast.

She stopped short on the landing. Her parents were standing in the lounge staring at something. She peered past them. They were looking at a jigsaw puzzle, and they turned to her as she entered the room.

'Phoebe,' her mum said, 'were you downstairs in the night? This puzzle was half-finished when we went to bed, now it's completed.'

Her parents enjoyed jigsaw puzzles. It was one of the ways they liked to relax after a busy day dealing with the bereaved. They had obviously been working at this one after Phoebe and Alex went to bed.

Her mum took her hand. 'Have you been sleepwalking again, Phoebe?' she asked.

When she was younger Phoebe had been a regular sleepwalker, leaving her bed at night, and wandering around the house. Her mother would find her asleep on the sofa when she came down in the morning, and on one occasion she'd climbed into the dog's basket and snuggled down with their very surprised Labrador, Sherlock.

'I don't think so,' Phoebe replied. 'But would I actually know if I *had* been sleepwalking? I don't think I knew before. I just used to wake up somewhere that wasn't my bed, and then go back upstairs to my room. Unless you found me first, of course.'

'Well, what other explanation could there be?'

Her dad laughed. Well, it was what passed for a laugh with her dad: a slight chuckle, almost like he was clearing his throat. Neither of Phoebe's parents were ever going to win gold medals in any laughing Olympics. In fact, they'd never come anywhere near being contestants in the first place. Their faces were sad, more often than not. It went with the job.

'Well, there's a couple of elderly gentlemen laid out in the funeral parlour,' her dad suggested. 'Perhaps one of them came back to life.'

Phoebe's mother glared at him. She didn't like him talking about things like that, especially in front of Phoebe. 'Go and get your breakfast, Richard,' she told him.

'I'm going to have to keep a careful eye on you for the next few nights,' she continued, turning back to Phoebe. 'I just can't imagine how you managed to complete that jigsaw without waking up, but for now, it's the only explanation.'

As she left the room, Phoebe's mum gave the puzzle one more glance, perhaps hoping to find a clue to the mystery, but nothing presented itself.

For Phoebe, however, there was no mystery. It could only have been Walter on his nighttime rambles. He'd obviously found the puzzle and whiled away the time putting the missing pieces in place.

On Thursday evening, Walter was back with Alex, but again he was restless, having already slept most of the day in Alex's rucksack.

He floated up to the windowsill and sat there looking down on the street. The moon was almost full, and after a while he saw two figures sneaking along in the darkness, keeping close to the houses. They were dressed in black, and both stopped by the wall that surrounded the garden. Then one knelt down, while the other climbed on his back and hauled himself onto the top of the wall. Then the climber reached down and helped the second figure to climb up, till both were seated astride the wall.

'Alex,' hissed Walter. '*Alex!* Come and look.'

Alex padded over to the window, and both watched the two figures preparing to jump down into the yard.

'This doesn't look good,' said Alex sleepily. 'I should tell my parents. You'd better hide, Walter, in case they come in here to take a look themselves.'

Mr Mitchell was annoyed at having to leave his favourite TV programme, but eventually Alex convinced him that he wasn't playing games, and that he really should come and see for himself. He was glad that he did. He could clearly make out both figures by the back door to the funeral parlour. He picked up Alex's phone and dialled 999.

It didn't take long before a police car arrived, and Mr Mitchell was able to show them exactly where to look for the intruders. Phoebe and Alex had joined him on the street, and they were just in time to see the two figures being escorted from the garden. They were none other than Frank and Rafe, who presumably had been hoping for a date with the recently deceased, but were now squealing and squirming in the grip of a policeman.

CHAPTER ELEVEN

It had been a long week with Walter, trying to keep him safe and out of trouble, and to make sure that no one found out about him, but finally it was Friday, and at 5:30pm the fish and chip van would be outside the churchyard.

Walter was sitting on the church wall after another unsuccessful attempt at taking him back through the gate. He hadn't been too keen to try more than once this time.

'Actually, I quite like living with you two,' he said, once he'd returned to his normal size again. 'There's nothing so great about the churchyard, particularly with Ned around. I've managed to stay clear of him for the past three hundred years, but I'm sure he's going to surprise me one day.'

'But what can he do to you?' asked Phoebe.

'He wants to kill me!' Walter replied.

'But how can he kill you if you're already dead?'

'I'm not sure, but believe me, he'll find a way. He's so furious with me for cutting short his life. He won't give up until he's done something awful to me.'

'Can't you apologise to him, say how sorry you are for causing his death? Maybe it's all that's needed,' said Phoebe.

'I think I should,' Walter replied. 'Problem is that I'm frightened of getting anywhere near him!'

'Do you think he'll talk to us?' Alex asked.

'I just don't know. He'll be amazed if you can see him, I know that. He hasn't had any human contact since he's been a ghost.'

'Tell us what he looks like.'

'He's a large man, a stout man. He was always very fond of food. He'd sample all the dishes that were cooked in his kitchen before they were sent to the table, and if something wasn't right he'd throw a tantrum. I once saw him get so angry with one of the kitchen staff that he tipped a bowl of stew over his head. The poor lad just stood there, covered in meat and vegetables, and dripping with gravy. Then Ned told him to lick it all up with his tongue.'

Alex and Phoebe looked at each other, eyes wide. Did they *really* want to meet Ned?

'I remember once when the surgeon came to pull out one of his teeth,' Walter continued. 'Ned had terrible toothache, but he was even more terrified of having it pulled out. He drank himself into a state where he didn't know what was happening, but it still took four stable lads to hold him down till the job was done. I can still hear him screaming at them.

'Watch out for his rolling pin too! He always has it

in his hand. I don't think he'll be able to hurt you with it, but best to stay clear, just in case.'

'Is there *anything* nice about him?' Alex asked breathlessly. Perhaps it would be easier if Walter just stayed in his wardrobe forever?

'He was better when he was with Agnes, his girlfriend, but once she moved away to work at Northmead Castle, he was angry all the time. Although there was one thing, I suppose. He loved dogs. He'd go really soppy when the two big dogs from the house found their way into his kitchen. He fed them, of course, so they kept coming back for more. He'd sit in a chair while he stroked them. He adored those dogs.'

'Wait here,' said Alex, inspiration striking him. 'I'll go and get Sherlock. He might get Ned talking to us.'

After Mrs Mitchell had got over the shock of Alex actually volunteering to walk the dog, he was soon back again. Sherlock looked immensely pleased to be out of the house.

Just then, they heard the noise of the fish and chip van as it rounded the corner of the churchyard and headed towards its usual stop by the back wall. 'Ned will be waiting for it,' said Walter. 'It's now or never.'

Phoebe, Alex and Sherlock slipped through the gate, Phoebe calling back to Walter to make sure he waited for them on the wall. They walked along a shady path between the gravestones. Sherlock paused to lift his leg now and then, but Phoebe kept pulling him away, telling him it was disrespectful.

They soon reached the churchyard wall between them and the fish and chip van. Both children and dog could smell the heavenly aroma wafting over. But where was Ned?

Maybe Walter was wrong. Maybe Ned wasn't always here, or maybe they just couldn't see him. Walter had said that he thought the only people who could see ghosts were the ones who wanted to see them. Did they *really* want to see Ned though? Perhaps they could have done without all of Walter's warnings. Now they were here, they supposed there was nothing else for it. They sat down with Sherlock and waited.

Five, maybe ten minutes passed by before they suddenly became aware of a slight movement from behind a large tree. It was like a patch of brown mist, roughly human in shape and height, and as they kept staring at it, its resemblance to a rather large human figure became clearer. Finally, they could make out the shape of a man. Sherlock had seen the figure too, and the hackles had risen on the back of his neck. He gave a low growl, which soon developed into a series of barks.

'So you can see me?' It was a gruff voice, but not totally unfriendly.

'Yes, we can see you,' Alex managed.

The next sound they heard was completely unexpected. It was the sound of sobbing. As far as they could tell from Ned's misty form, he had his hands over his eyes and his whole body was shaking.

When he finally calmed down, Phoebe said, 'We're really sorry, we didn't mean to upset you.'

'It just came over me, I can't help it. It was a shock. You're the first people I've spoken to since I passed over. I was overcome, knowing that you could see me. I've been so miserable for nigh on three hundred years now. I've been cold and lonely. You see, I didn't lead a very good life, and I've had plenty of time to think about it. This can only be punishment for the way I was.'

Alex noticed that Sherlock had calmed down at the sound of Ned's voice. In fact, he was pulling on the lead, wanting to move closer to him.

'Can I... Can I stroke your dog?' Ned asked shyly.

'Of course.'

Sherlock rolled over onto his back, into his favourite position where his tummy could be rubbed. It seemed that even as a ghost, Ned still had a way with dogs. Phoebe was thinking how bizarre this all was. Only five days previously, they had been blissfully unaware of ghosts in any shape or form. Since then, not only had they taken one home with them, but they were now talking to another, watching him fuss their dog. Nobody, absolutely nobody, would believe it if they told them.

'How did you know I was here?' asked Ned. 'I know enough of the ghost world to know that a ghost can only be seen by someone who wants to see one, someone whose mind is open to the possibility.'

'Walter told us you'd be here.'

They sensed momentary anger at the mention of Walter's name. 'He's the reason I'm here,' Ned whispered. 'Has he told you what happened?'

'Yes, he has, and he's really sorry about it.' Phoebe crossed her fingers. She didn't actually know if that was true, but the meeting with Ned was going so well that she thought a little white lie might be OK.

'Where is he? Every time I try to get near him, he disappears. I'm past caring about what happened now. Three hundred years is a long time to hold a grudge, a long time to mull things over too. There's nothing that can be done to change what happened.'

Just then they caught a very strong whiff of fish and chips. Ned groaned. 'What I'd give to be able to have just one plate of that fabulous food. That's what I miss the most.'

'We need to ask you something,' said Alex. 'Can you leave the churchyard, or are you stuck here?'

'I can't leave,' said Ned. 'I've tried. It's hopeless.'

'The problem we have is that we managed to get Walter out by taking him with us, but now we can't get him back in. We thought you might be able to help.'

It sounded like Ned was chuckling to himself. 'What makes you think I'd want him back here?'

'We know you have every reason not to want him back, and we quite understand that, but we can't look after him forever, and we've no idea what will happen if he doesn't get back in!'

It seemed as if Ned was losing interest in the conversation, his shape becoming less clear, then indistinct till all that was left of him was his voice.

It sounded like he was singing.

Suddenly they both became aware that Walter was sitting on the churchyard wall. He'd kept out of sight on the other side while Ned was around, but now he had floated up and was pushing hard against the invisible barrier.

'I just don't know whether to believe Ned,' he said. 'Has he really forgiven me?'

It was at that moment, just as Alex and Phoebe were weighing their replies, that it happened. Something that took everyone completely by surprise. Rafe and Frank appeared on the wall, either side of Walter, and quickly slipped a bin bag over him. Just as quickly they jumped down again, but the bin bag wouldn't shift. They tugged and tugged till suddenly it came free, and both boys flew backwards onto the ground.

Alex and Phoebe were horrified. Not only could Rafe and Frank see Walter, but they'd got him, they'd captured him, they'd trapped him in a bin bag!

'What do we do now?' said Alex, looking mournfully at Phoebe.

Close by, a small voice whispered, 'We go home. Surely they didn't think I couldn't get free from a bag! Didn't they look funny, falling on their bums!'

CHAPTER TWELVE

The weekend was quiet. Well, perhaps not *quiet* exactly. Walter spent much of Saturday adding songs to his heavy metal playlist, although his favourite was still 'Highway to Hell'. He had it on repeat, and by the end of the day Mrs Mitchell told Alex she couldn't stand to hear that song again.

Phoebe and Alex's parents were the sort of parents who thought that Sunday was a wasted day if you didn't spend it visiting somewhere interesting. But the twins knew by now that their idea of somewhere interesting was rarely the same as their parents'.

Sometimes they both found it difficult to talk to their dad. He was often sad, as if something awful had happened or was about to happen. Alex had heard their mum talking to a friend once, something about his dad having Seasonal Affective Disorder, or SAD for short. Alex didn't think that his sadness was seasonal – he seemed to be sad all year round. It affected their mum too. She smiled, but behind the smile was concern and worry about her husband.

As they climbed into the car, their mum said, 'I'm

glad we're going to Northmead Castle, the gardens are sure to be lovely.'

The gardens are sure to be boring, thought Alex.

'It's supposed to have a ghost,' said Phoebe.

'A ghost?' a small voice crackled. Fortunately, neither of their parents heard.

Alex whispered to Phoebe, 'Where is he?'

'In my bag.'

'I hope you warned him to stay silent.'

'I did.'

And now it was late afternoon, and they were all sitting in the almost empty tea rooms. Here Alex and Phoebe suffered another disappointment. They were out of chocolate cake.

It had been the thought of a large slice of delicious chocolate cake that had got them through the afternoon. First they'd trailed around the castle, looking at room after room filled with four poster beds. Next they'd dawdled in the gardens and failed to get excited about the wonderful flowers that their parents showed them.

Finally, they'd come to the tea rooms, Alex racing ahead of them to get to his favourite seat by a window that overlooked the lake. Then their dad had broken the bad news.

Alex and Phoebe picked at the lemon slices that had been bought for them and stared at the lake.

'Why don't you go off and explore for a bit?' said their dad. 'There's still an hour before we need to leave.'

As they left the tea rooms, they heard Walter's voice

from Alex's pocket. 'Where's the ghost? I've been peeping out from your bag all afternoon, and I've seen nothing. I want to see if this ghost knows any way of leaving the castle. And if he ever *has* left, how he found his way back in again. If it works for him, it might work for me.'

They found themselves heading towards the great hall. There was no one else about and the place seemed cavernous. Alex cupped his hands and called out, 'HULLO...' The echo rolled around the room.

They started to play a game where they had to avoid treading on cracks in the flagstone floor. They managed to cross successfully from one side of the hall to the other, but then Walter called out, 'I can see something!'

He floated free of Phoebe's bag and upward towards a balcony. As they watched, Alex and Phoebe could both begin to make out a misty shape forming, coalescing into something that looked human, or rather something that could have previously been human. There was a definite green tinge to the shape too.

Then they heard a voice. 'My, you're a cute little boy. How come I've never seen you around here before?'

Then they heard Walter. 'I don't actually live here. No, that's wrong. What I mean is, I didn't actually die here. I've travelled here from another place.'

They heard a chuckle. 'I've never heard of a ghost doing that before. *We* certainly can't leave the castle.'

Phoebe and Alex found that they could suddenly see this ghost very clearly. She was wearing a long flowing green dress and had green feathers in her hair.

Her next question surprised them. 'Do you sing?' she asked Walter.

'Yes, I do sing a bit,' Walter said.

'Well, now you're here, you could join our choir. We sing each night. There are six of us here and it passes the time. As you must know, time passes very slowly when you're a ghost. I remember being bored as a child and thinking how slowly time passed, but believe me, that was nothing compared to years, decades, centuries of time ebbing away.'

'What sort of songs do you sing?'

Alex and Phoebe glanced at each other. Both knew what was coming next.

'Do you know "Highway to Hell"?' asked Walter.

'I don't think so,' said the green lady. 'Sisters,' she called out, 'do any of you know a song called "Highway to Hell"?'

Alex and Phoebe could see more shapes forming around the green lady – reds, greys and whites – till the whole choir appeared there on the balcony looking down at them.

'It's sung by AC/DC,' said Walter, trying to be helpful.

There was a sound of dry rasping voices all talking at once. Then the green lady answered, 'We don't seem to know that song. We don't think it was ever sung at the village church. The vicar always used to go on about the fires of Hell, how we needed to live good lives or risk eternal damnation, but I don't think we ever sang songs about it.'

At that moment Walter broke into his own version of the song, complete with air guitar pyrotechnics. It was rocky and noisy and very energetic. The ghostly figures seemed to take a step backwards. There were lots of voices, lots of protestations:

'No, no, no!'

'That's far too loud!'

'It's not just loud, it's hurting my ears!'

'Make him stop!'

'Never heard anything like it!'

'Send him away!'

'Oh, but he's so cute,' said the original green lady. 'Why don't we ask him to stay and teach him some much nicer songs. It would be lovely to have a young ghost in our midst. He'd help us pass the time.'

'Well, thank you,' said Walter, 'but I need to go back to my home. What I would like to know, though, is how come there are so many of you here?'

'We all have unfinished business. Our lives were cut short. Tell him, sisters.'

'I fell from the balcony.'

'I drowned in the moat.'

'I was murdered by my husband.'

'I broke my neck when I fell from my horse.'

'The plague did it for me.'

Their voices sounded so sad. Walter, they hoped, would liven things up for them.

'Oh, please stay,' they pleaded.

'Make him stay!'

'Don't go.'

'We'll look after you.'

'We'll mother you, keep you safe.'

'Do stay with us.'

Walter shook his head and floated down to the ground. It was obvious to everyone that this choir of ghostly ladies had no idea as to how ghosts might leave or enter the place they were haunting.

'At the very least,' called the green lady, 'won't you come back tonight and listen to our singing? We don't get much of an audience. A few foxes join in but they're not very tuneful.'

Just at that moment their parents entered the hall, looking for Phoebe and Alex. Walter quickly disappeared into Phoebe's bag.

As Mr and Mrs Mitchell herded them back out towards the car, they sneaked a look up at the balcony, but there was nothing to be seen.

Alex wondered if anyone else had ever travelled home from a castle with a pocket full of ghost, but he didn't wonder for long. A smell suddenly filled the car, the same smell that had caused everyone to evacuate the classroom earlier that week.

Alex and Phoebe looked at each other in horror.

'It must be coming in from outside,' said Mr Mitchell. 'Close the windows.'

Buttons were pushed, but with all the windows closed the smell was much, *much* worse.

'Stop the car!' Mrs Mitchell pleaded.

They pulled into the edge of the road, where doors were opened and everyone breathed in deep lungfuls of air. 'That wasn't you, was it, Alex?' their dad asked. He'd always say that when they passed a pig farm or field of cabbages.

'No, it wasn't,' Alex replied in a hurt voice. 'As if anyone could think that it was.'

He walked round to the back of the car and hissed at Walter.

'That was you again, wasn't it?'

'I'm afraid it was. All that movement at high speed. It must have done something to me.'

'How do you feel now? Do you think we can get back in the car and go home?' he asked Walter.

'I think I should be all right now, I feel much more comfortable.'

Mr Mitchell had the bonnet up on the car and was peering at the engine as if it might be to blame. He tutted and shook his head, but eventually was forced to close it again, and they all got back inside.

'Well,' said Alex, when he and Phoebe were back home, 'the problem still remains. How do we get Walter back into the churchyard?'

'If I have a problem,' said Phoebe, 'I usually Google it, but I don't think that will be of any help this time.'

Alex shrugged. 'It's worth a try,' he said. 'It's not like I have any better ideas.'

Alex typed 'Ghosts' into the search bar.

Wikipedia had a lot about ghosts, and Phoebe, looking at the screen over his shoulder, was drawn to a line that read: 'Hunters can't agree on what a ghost is, or offer proof that they exist. It's all speculation and guesswork.'

'Well,' she said, 'we know something they don't.'

She also read that some scientists believe that ghosts are spirits of the dead who get 'lost' on their way to 'the other side'.

'That's Walter's theory too,' said Alex.

Walter, who had been quiet up to that point, suddenly spoke up. 'I wonder if one of those ladies at the castle was Ned's girlfriend.'

Alex and Phoebe looked at each other but didn't say anything. It seemed a complication that neither of them needed just at that moment.

CHAPTER THIRTEEN

'Mr Khan, Mr Khan…'

Rafe was calling out across the playground, but it seemed like his teacher was suffering from temporary loss of hearing. In fact, he was moving away from Rafe, and striking up a conversation with someone's mum who had accompanied her daughter into school that morning.

'Mr Khan, Mr Khan…'

The teacher broke off from his conversation and turned around. 'Rafe, I am talking. Wait quietly till I'm finished.'

Waiting quietly was not something Rafe was good at. He shuffled around, shifting from one foot to the other, keeping in his teacher's sightline till Mr Khan ended his conversation and reluctantly called the boy forward.

'What is the matter, Rafe?'

Alex and Phoebe edged nearer. What Rafe said was often amusing, and their teacher's response, even more so.

'Mr Khan, Alex and Phoebe have got a pet ghost.

I've seen it. I almost caught it yesterday, but it can get out of bin bags. They keep it in Phoebe's pencil case. I knew there was something funny going on. Take a look in her case if you don't believe me.'

Alex looked nervously at Phoebe, but they couldn't help but smile when they heard their teacher's reply.

'Rafe, I've listened to some very strange things from you, but this must be the strangest of all. Are you sure you are well?'

'It's true, it's true! Have a look in Phoebe's pencil case if you don't believe me.'

Alex felt something move in his pocket and realised that Walter had left the pencil case for a safer hiding place, just in case Mr Khan took Rafe seriously.

'Rafe, I have no intention of searching through Phoebe's pencil case in response to your wild imaginings. Just listen to what you're saying. You are no stranger to tall tales and porky pies, but this one is beyond belief.'

'But it's true, it's true! Just look.'

Rafe's voice was getting louder and louder. Finally, he ran to Phoebe, grabbed her pencil case, unzipped it and let the contents fall to the floor. Then he was on his knees sifting through her pencils and pens like an old-time gold prospector expecting to find precious metal. Finally, he was forced to give up. He glared up at Phoebe. 'Where is it?'

'Where's what, Rafe?' Phoebe answered.

'Your ghost.'

'Rafe, do you know how ridiculous you sound? I don't know what you're looking for.'

'You *do* know what I'm looking for, and he does too,' Rafe said, pointing at Alex. 'You've found something and you're keeping it secret. It's just not fair.'

'Life isn't fair, Rafe,' said Mr Khan. 'It isn't fair that I have to suffer you in my class every day. Now please go away and bother someone else with your daft stories.'

'I'll find your ghost,' Rafe said. 'I'll find it and then you'll all be sorry that you didn't believe me.'

Phoebe and Alex looked at each other. Maybe this wasn't quite the right moment to talk to Mr Khan about Walter after all.

After school that evening Alex and Phoebe were sitting on the church wall. Walter, almost back to his normal size, sat between them.

Alex was continuing his enquiries about what had happened to Walter when he'd fallen from the roof.

'So after you realised you were a ghost, what happened next?'

'It was a very strange time. I still seemed to have human feelings, even though I wasn't alive anymore. I felt incredibly sad, and lonely too. I was hiding to begin with, trying to keep out of Ned's way, and then I watched my own funeral. It was a dreadful day, the rain was pouring down, and there were my family all gathered together around the grave. My mother was weeping, and all I wanted to do was reach out and touch her, but I couldn't.'

'Oh, Walter, that must have been horrible,' said Phoebe, wiping her eyes with her sleeve.

'It was such a long time ago now. I remember those feelings, but I don't have them anymore. I am what I am, and that's life – or rather death, I suppose.'

'I suppose you must have a gravestone with your name on somewhere in the churchyard,' said Alex.

'I do, although it has weathered a lot down the years, and much of the writing on it is difficult to read, but you can still see my name.'

'Where is it? Can we see it?'

'It's over there,' Walter said. 'But you'll have to find it yourselves, of course.'

Phoebe and Alex jumped down from the wall and set off in the direction that Walter had pointed to.

After a bit of rummaging through long grass and undergrowth, they found the stone quite easily.

'Hey, Walter,' Alex called excitedly, 'your surname, Mitchell, is the same as ours!'

'Yes,' Walter called back. 'I seem to remember that it was a common name in the village when I was a child.'

'But it's amazing!' exclaimed Phoebe. 'We might

even be related. You could be one of our ancestors, maybe our great, great, great, several more times great uncle. That's got to be a reason to help you.'

'While you're in there,' said Walter, 'I think you should talk to Minnie. She was a teacher. If anyone knows a way to get in and out of the churchyard, it will be her. She was always teaching us local history. We should find her.'

'Where do we find her?' Alex asked.

'Well...' Walter hesitated. 'That's the tricky bit. The main problem is that she's always asleep. She was quite old when she died. She rests in one of the vaults at the back of the churchyard, and I've only ever seen her out and about on four or five occasions in the last three hundred years.'

'Can we wake her?'

'You can, but I'm not sure how she'd take it. I think I'd have to wake her myself and then try to explain the situation before she'd be ready to meet you.'

'But you can't get back into the churchyard,' Phoebe pointed out.

Walter had obviously overlooked this small but important detail.

'Wait a minute,' said Alex excitedly, after a moment's thought, 'couldn't we ask Ned to wake her?'

'We could try, but Ned doesn't like her very much. When they were both alive, she kept telling him off for his rough manners and bad behaviour.'

'But what other way is there?'

'There isn't,' Walter admitted. 'It's our only hope.'

'So,' said Alex, 'we have four days before the fish and chip van appears again, to prepare some convincing reasons to put to Ned as to why he should wake Minnie. Life was so much simpler for us, Walter, before we met you.'

'Absolutely no way,' said Ned, after they'd tracked him down the following Friday. 'I've got nothing to gain from it. I'm stuck here, going nowhere, and while I'm stuck, I want a simple life, or what passes for a life, thank you very much.'

'But you *have* got something to gain,' called Walter from the church wall, where he was leaning against the invisible barrier. 'If we can discover a way to leave the churchyard, we might all be able to pass on to the next stage of our afterlife. There's got to be more to death than just hanging around here forever.'

'There is,' said Ned. 'We're the ones who missed out when the gates opened. You see, there are places where the left behinds, like us, can pass through to the next stage of our existence in the afterlife. Most people pass through OK when they die, but for some reason we didn't. Maybe we dawdled, or we failed to notice where everyone else was going, and by the time we reached the right place the gates had closed and left us here.'

'But where are these gates?' Phoebe asked.

'I've no idea,' said Ned. 'All I know is what Minnie once told me. She seems to think that at certain times of day, the boundary between this world and the next is likely to be thinned, and that there are certain places where a ghost might pass through.'

'That's why we need to talk to Minnie,' said Walter. 'Maybe she'll know where those places are. Maybe we can travel there together.'

Ned was obviously, or had obviously been, the sort of person who takes time to think things through. Phoebe recognised that in herself, and from living with their dad, who rarely answered straight away when there was a problem to be solved. He'd think about it for days sometimes, till it seemed as if he'd never make up his mind, and then suddenly, when all the planets had realigned themselves and the moon was in the right position – well, that was how their mum described it – he'd say what he thought. If their mum didn't agree with him, she'd try and persuade him to change his mind. Sometimes it worked, sometimes it didn't, and sometimes it took just as long again for Dad to weigh up the pros and cons of her argument.

Ned was keeping very quiet, and Phoebe wondered if they'd have to wait a whole week, till the fish and chip van came round again, before he'd give his reply.

After what seemed like an eternity, Ned said, 'Well, I suppose it might be worth my while. I don't really want to stay here forever. Follow me.'

Ned led Phoebe and Alex across the churchyard towards the back wall, where there was a rectangular stone tomb. Walter made a quick circuit of the walls until he was on the section behind the tomb, where Ned thought that Minnie might be found.

As they were standing there, Ned suddenly looked as if he was having second thoughts. He looked very worried and started pacing up and down. 'She doesn't like me,' he said. 'She's never liked me.'

'Listen, Ned,' said Alex, 'I can't imagine that she likes being stuck here anymore than you do. She might actually be pleased with you if she thinks that you both have a chance to move on.'

'Well, there is that, I suppose.'

After a few moments chewing it over, Ned made a decision and knelt down by the side of the tomb. Phoebe and Alex could hear him calling, 'Miss Minnie, Miss Minnie, wake up!'

It seemed to take forever till they heard another voice, a sleepy voice, a grumpy voice. 'Oh, it's you, Ned. What do you want? Why are you disturbing my sleep? I've told you before I don't want to be woken. The only time I'm happy is when I'm asleep, so you'd better have a good reason for this.'

'Well, ma'am, I'm truly sorry I needed to wake you, but Walter and I think we should make another effort to leave the churchyard and move on. You see, we have some help this time.'

'Help? Help? What do you mean by help? Who have you shown yourself to? You know we agreed to keep hidden away. I can't believe you've been so stupid. Don't you realise that if word gets out that there are three ghosts in this churchyard, there'll be crowds of people looking for us. They'll find us too, and we'll end up being exhibited in some freak show. People will come to gawk at us, and we won't get a moment's peace. Oh, I just can't believe you've done this, Ned. You had very little intelligence when you were a child, and now you seem to have lost what little you ever had.'

'It's not what you think, ma'am.' Ned's voice again. 'There are two children here and I think they can be trusted.'

'Trusted? Never.' Minnie really sounded angry now. 'Children can never be trusted, they can't keep secrets, ever.'

'Actually, I think these ones can. They found Walter a couple of weeks back and somehow managed to get him out of the churchyard.'

'That's impossible. How on earth did they do that?'

'I don't know how, but they did, and now he

can't get back in. Walter thinks that these two young friends of his can help us find the gates where we can pass through.'

'Let me see these children. From what I remember of the children I taught, most of them were nasty little brats. I couldn't stand them.'

Waiting outside, Alex and Phoebe began to feel very cold. They thought back to the time when they'd first met Walter, and how they'd felt an icy chill as he passed through them. They were feeling the same sensation again now. Suddenly it went and they felt warmer again. Presumably they'd been inspected by Minnie.

Then they heard her voice again. 'There is a place, a special place, a holy place where I suspect we might find some gates. I was taken there once as a child. It was a circle of standing stones, huge stones, and the dying rays of the sun seemed to spotlight them. If anywhere's the place, I bet it's there. And I know just when we'd need to be there, a time when surely the gates would open and let us through.'

'What's this place called?' Ned asked, 'Do you remember?'

'I do. It seems to have stuck in my mind. It's called Stonehenge. And we need to be there at sunset or sunrise.'

'I've seen it,' said Alex. 'We drove past it once when we were going on holiday. It looked amazing.'

'So now we have two problems,' said Alex to

Phoebe. 'Firstly, how do Ned and Minnie get out of the churchyard, and secondly, how on earth do we get them to Stonehenge?'

'Actually,' a voice behind them said, 'you have three problems.'

They spun round to find Rafe clutching his phone. 'I had hoped to photograph one ghost, but it looks like I've snapped three of them! Our two friends here plus another on the wall. Mr Khan will have to believe me now!'

He turned and fist-pumped the air before racing off.

CHAPTER FOURTEEN

'Tell me,' said Mr Khan, the next morning before school started. 'Tell me there's some logical explanation to these photographs that Rafe has shown me.'

Alex and Phoebe had arrived early, hoping to catch their teacher before Rafe had a chance to show him the photograph, but Rafe had beaten them to it.

'I had Rafe rush in here like a mini tornado and thrust his phone at me,' Mr Khan continued. 'He has photographs of three ghosts, or so he says, which he claims to have taken in the churchyard. Please tell me that he's Photoshopped them in some way. Do tell me they're not real, because they looked real enough to me.'

Phoebe looked at Alex, who was staring at the floor, then spoke very quietly.

'We can't tell you that, because it is the truth. Rafe's camera didn't lie. There are three ghosts in the churchyard.'

'If I didn't know you better,' their teacher said, 'I'd be tempted to think that you'd teamed up with Rafe to play some elaborate trick on me. But it's not April Fools' Day, and I know it's something you wouldn't do. It's just that I'm astounded. I don't know what to say or think. I'm in complete shock. Has Rafe shown these photos to anyone else? No, that's a silly question, of course he has. I've never known Rafe to keep quiet about anything before, let alone something like this.'

'But will anyone believe him?' Alex asked. 'You only believe us because you trust us to tell you the truth. Would anyone trust Rafe?'

'That's a good question. But it's not the only one. What I want to know is what happens to these ghosts now?' asked Mr Khan.

'We need to take them to Stonehenge,' Phoebe replied. 'They think it could be a way out of this world and a gateway to the next stage of their afterlives.'

'I've never heard that before, but then again nobody really knows why Stonehenge was built or what it was for.'

At that moment the classroom door burst open and Rafe stormed in, followed by a mob of children.

'Can we all go ghost hunting, Mr Khan? We've got to find them. We'll be famous! We can get the TV people round to interview them. It'll be amazing!'

'Rafe,' called out Mr Khan, 'we are about to begin the school day. Sit down and be quiet. I don't want to hear any more about the matter. I'll take your phone too, Rafe. You know you're not allowed to have a phone in school.'

Reluctantly Rafe handed over the phone. 'Don't think you can delete the pictures and that will be that. I've already uploaded them onto my computer. You should see them on a bigger screen!'

All day long Rafe went on and on about the pictures to anyone who would listen. He kept saying that he was going to sell them to the newspapers, and how he was sure they'd pay him a large sum of money for them. He talked about all the things he'd say when they came to interview him and how he'd probably be on national television. He'd be the boy who'd proven that ghosts were real. Mr Khan told him on several occasions, and in various ways, to be quiet, to put a sock in it, to stop bleating. Then finally he lost his temper, came up close to Rafe, and in a voice that sounded quietly menacing, ordered him out of the room.

Phoebe and Alex didn't know where Rafe spent the rest of the day, or who was having to put up with him. They were just glad that he wasn't bothering them.

Mr Khan was in a better temper with Rafe absent, although he looked very thoughtful during the class's 'Drop Everything and Read' time. Usually he looked as if he were lost in the book he was reading, but on this occasion he just looked lost. *He is probably trying to process what he's seen in Rafe's photos,* Alex thought.

When school was over, Rafe was waiting by the gate, and it turned out that he'd spent his time in isolation thinking very hard about what to do with his photos. It seemed that he'd changed his mind about sending them to the papers and had come up with what he thought was a much better plan. The photos had given him bargaining power, and he was about to use it.

Phoebe and Alex walked off, with Rafe closely following behind them.

'Hey, you two,' he called out, 'wait a minute, I have an idea.' They paused while he caught up with them. Whatever his idea was, both Phoebe and Alex knew it wouldn't be something they'd want to go along with. At the same time, what choice did they have but to hear him out?

'I won't show these photographs to the paper if you let me come round to your place, Phoebe, and lift up the lid on a coffin.'

By the time Alex had thought of a polite way to say 'No', it was too late. He watched in shock as Phoebe, his usually quiet and often introspective sister, transformed into a whirling tornado of fury heading straight towards Rafe. He'd never seen her like this before.

Neither had Rafe, who was about to experience what it felt like to be sucked into a maelstrom and spat back out again. Phoebe attacked him with clenched hands and kicking feet. She jumped on his back and forced him to the ground, all the while beating him about the body. Rafe found himself unable to escape until Alex intervened and pulled Phoebe away from him.

Rafe stood up and shook himself. Once he'd got his breath back, he muttered, 'Well, there's no need for that. I only asked a simple question.'

'What part of "No!" don't you understand, Rafe?' Phoebe spat out the words as if they were venom and she was a hissing cobra. 'You will never, I repeat *never*, do that. I don't care what you do with the photographs, but what you ask is off-limits.'

'Well, if that's a non-starter, how about asking the ghosts to find me a hand of glory. There must be one somewhere, and I bet they know where it is. I bet it's in one of those old tombs at the very back of the churchyard.'

So that was it. Rafe must have heard Walter's whisper that time in the classroom.

'We'll think about it, Rafe,' said Alex, over his shoulder, as he dragged Phoebe behind him, down the street.

'You'd better not think about it for too long,' Rafe said, scrambling after them. 'In fact, I'd better put a time limit on this. Let's say tomorrow after school. We'll meet in the churchyard and have a look around. By then you'll have had time to talk to your ghostly friends and find out where it is. And you'd better make sure they know what will happen if they don't cooperate. There'll be ghosthunters swarming all over the gravestones!'

When they arrived back home, they found Walter still sleeping, but he soon woke up once Alex turned the volume of his phone up to LOUD and blasted out 'Highway to Hell'.

Walter jerked into life and started playing air guitar. They let him have his moment of pleasure before explaining what had happened at school. Then they asked if there really was a hand of glory in the churchyard.

'There is,' Walter said with a nod. 'It was the hand of a highwayman and a thief who was hanged at the crossroads just outside the village. They hung criminals there because it was where four roads met. They thought that if the highwayman's ghost appeared he would be confused by the four roads and not know which direction to take, so the ghost would stay by the gallows and eventually fade away.

'It was considered great entertainment to be taken to see the hanging back then. My family all went, even my mother. A lot of people turned up because they'd been robbed by him or he'd murdered someone they knew. Nobody felt any sympathy for him. He was locked in a cage when they hung him, and then left there for crows to peck at his eyes and strip away his flesh. His hand was removed while his body was still warm.'

'What did they do with it?'

'Well, somehow it must have made its way into the

churchyard. It's behind the tomb where Minnie rests in the big mausoleum. Rats must have gnawed away at it over the years, so there's not much left apart from bone. If it had any magical properties, they must have disappeared long ago.'

'Rafe will be disappointed,' said Alex. 'He's counting on it working for him.' Turning to Phoebe he added, 'It's probably better for everyone if it doesn't though. I suppose it won't hurt to show Rafe where it is, and it might buy us some time while he tries to find out what he can do with it – or more likely, what he *can't* do with it.'

The next afternoon, they met up at the churchyard. Phoebe and Alex were there along with Rafe and his mate Frank. Rafe had a torch, a pair of gloves and a carrier bag to put the hand in. They'd left Walter watching from the churchyard wall, pushing every now and then at the invisible barrier that was still keeping him out.

Sunshine never seemed to reach the farthest part of the churchyard. The grass was always wet and the temperature several degrees lower than elsewhere. It had a gloomy, unattended feel to it. The gravestones were often leaning at crazy angles and covered in lichen. Weathering from wind and rain over the years meant that most of the lettering was impossible to read.

In the gloomiest corner, backed up to the churchyard wall, were a pair of mausoleums. Alex thought that they looked like garden sheds made of stone. The roofs and walls were mostly covered in ivy. The furthest one was surrounded by iron railings, but the one they needed to enter had just a gate across the entrance to the tomb.

A couple of decorated urns stood sentry-like on each side of the metal gate, and beyond them a pair of extremely gnarled trees that looked as if they were far older than the tombs themselves. There were plaques with faded inscriptions that would probably have given clues to the occupants had it been possible to decipher them.

Phoebe felt very uneasy. She'd read a number of vampire stories, and this part of the churchyard played on her imagination. If they started to hear scratching and clawing noises, as if something was trying to escape these burial places, she knew she wouldn't be hanging around to find out what it was.

Rafe, on the other hand, was quite happy. 'Frank,' he called out, 'let's see if we can shift the gate.'

They both put their shoulders to the gate and were encouraged to discover that there was a slight movement. They pushed again but something was stopping it shifting anymore. They dropped to their knees, put their arms between the bars of the gate and pulled out debris. A piece of wood had wedged itself under the gate and was acting like a door stop. They tugged at this until it came free.

Then, climbing back back onto their feet they

pushed again, and the gate opened enough to let them slip through. Then Rafe stuck his head back out. 'Come and see this!'

Alex and Phoebe looked at each other. They hadn't thought about having to follow Rafe into the darkness.

Reluctantly, they moved towards the tomb and peered inside. Frank's torch showed two arches which were fronted by iron railings. Beyond the railings were two stone coffins which presumably contained the tomb's occupants. Phoebe was relieved to see that there was no way for Rafe to get past the railings. He wouldn't be able to lift a lid and peer at whatever remains lay within.

Alex nudged her, pointing down at Rafe and Frank, who were on their knees again, this time peering around the floor of the tomb, presumably hoping to find the hand of glory.

Instead they discovered a stone slab set into the floor, with an iron ring attached to it. 'I bet it's underneath this,' Rafe said. 'Help me shift it, Frank.'

Before they could make a start, Frank, who had been feeling around behind the slab, put his hand on something that made him jump back. 'There's something there!'

Rafe felt in the same area then pulled his hand back quickly. 'Give me the gloves, Frank. If I'm not mistaken, this is what we're looking for.'

As Rafe eased out his discovery from behind the slab, Phoebe and Alex heard a rattling sound. It was the sound of the bones of a hand clicking together. Rafe held it aloft, a huge grin on his face. 'Well, look what it is, a hand of glory! I just knew I'd find it, I just knew. Now I've got to find out what I can do with it. Maybe for starters it will open this stone slab, so we can see what's beneath it.'

Then, brandishing his grisly discovery, Rafe hesitated. He'd found the hand, but how did he use it? Should he point it at the slab and command it to open? Were there some magic words that he needed to say. In *Aladdin*, you had to rub the lamp first and release a genie. He seemed to remember the words 'Open Sesame'.

Phoebe watched, hardly believing she was part of this, as he pointed the ghastly bones towards the stone slab. Nothing happened. Rafe shook them about a bit, held them one way then another. 'By the hand of glory,' his voice boomed, 'I command thee to open up!'

A couple of rooks in the trees outside flew up into the air, startled by the noise, but apart from that, nothing. The slab stayed firmly in position. 'What if we just try and pull the ring?' Frank asked. 'Maybe the hand will have made it easy for us.'

Rafe put the bones down, and both he and Frank took hold of the ring. Rafe counted to three and then both boys pulled as hard as they could. There was movement but not much. 'Hey,' Rafe called to Alex, 'get over here and help us.'

Alex didn't really want to be involved, but he took

hold of the ring, and after counting to three they all gave an almighty pull. The slab shifted and then tipped back, revealing a black hole with steps leading down into the darkness. Quickly Rafe grabbed the torch and shone it down the steps.

'Well,' he said, 'what have we here?'

CHAPTER FIFTEEN

Later that evening, Phoebe and Alex were talking to their dad. He liked looking into local history, and Phoebe said that if anyone would know about tunnels in the village, their dad would. They'd cornered him when he'd finished work and pretended that they were involved in a project at school.

'Well,' he said, sitting down in his favourite armchair and pulling off his shoes, 'as it happens, I do know something.

'The village was mixed up in smuggling for many years. I've pointed out the smugglers' graves in the churchyard, the ones marked with a skull and crossbones. There's a famous poem too, written by Rudyard Kipling, called 'The Smugglers' Song' which, if my memory is correct, has the lines:

Them that asks no questions isn't told a lie –
Watch the wall, my darling, while the Gentlemen go by!

'Do you know what Kipling meant by that?' he asked.

Alex looked puzzled, but Phoebe was quick to reply. 'He meant that people should turn a blind eye as to any crimes that were taking place. If they didn't, the smugglers would punish them, I suppose.'

'That's absolutely right. All kinds of people were involved. Over the years I've researched our family history, and it seems that our family was involved in the smuggling trade too. That's something that makes me sad, as I hate the thought of our family being descended from criminals, but it seems that in previous times, our family used to live in the big house beyond the churchyard, where they allowed the smugglers to store a lot of their illegal goods. They were found out eventually, and our ancestors were taken off to prison.

'They lost the big house and seemed to disappear from the village for many years, but then I found out that Mitchells returned and moved into our house, the old vicarage. That's when they set up the undertaking business, and Mitchells have lived in this house ever since.'

'So, do you know if there were any smugglers' tunnels in the village, Dad?' Alex asked.

Their parents looked at each other. 'I suppose they're old enough not to worry about it now. Perhaps we'd better tell them. What do you think?'

Their mum shrugged her shoulders. 'It's up to you.'

He got out of his seat and left the room. 'Follow me,' they heard him call.

They found him in the utility room tugging at a

carpet that covered most of the floor. He loosened it and began to roll it back.

Phoebe and Alex couldn't believe what they saw beneath the carpet. Set into the stone floor was a slab that was almost identical to the one they'd found in the mausoleum. A metal ring was set into a round groove in the slab, just like the one that Alex had helped Rafe and Frank pull earlier that day.

Their dad fetched a torch from the kitchen.

'We didn't tell you about this before,' he said, 'because we didn't want to worry you or give you nightmares thinking about it. You're old enough now to appreciate it as a bit of history.'

The slab was easier to pull open than the one in the churchyard, and when the torch was shone into the hole, there were steps leading down into darkness.

Walter, who up to that moment had been incredibly quiet in Alex's pocket, began to wriggle about. Suddenly he leapt out and began to grow very rapidly. Both Alex and Phoebe could see him, but even though their parents couldn't, they did hear a voice, a shrill voice, an excited voice saying, 'Wow! This must connect with the entrance in the tomb, and it might even let us go in and out of the churchyard!'

Alex and Phoebe both broke into a fit of coughing, but it couldn't disguise the fact that someone had spoken – and by the expression on their parents' faces, it was clear that they knew it wasn't any of them.

*

It was later that same evening, and they were sitting down again in the living room. Walter was sitting on the settee between Alex and Phoebe, and was gradually becoming visible to their parents.

At first their mum and dad had felt that some elaborate hoax was being played on them. Their dad said that he'd always had an open mind about ghosts, but despite dealing with the dead every day in his job, he had never found any reason to believe that they were anything but figments of someone's imagination. He looked shocked, as if his whole world had been turned upside down. Their mum had gone 'as white as a sheet', to use a cliché that Alex and Phoebe were always being told to avoid using in their writing at school. In this instance, however, it described exactly what she looked like.

Phoebe and Alex had spent a long time telling their parents the whole story, how they'd found Walter and how they hadn't been able to get him back into the churchyard. They explained how Rafe had photographed Walter on his phone, and how Mr Khan had also seen the photograph.

Then had come an even trickier moment, when they had revealed that there were two more ghosts in the churchyard.

Their dad's last words, as Phoebe and Alex went to bed that night, were: 'We're going to have to sleep on this one, see what it looks like in the morning.'

Alex thought to himself that it probably wouldn't

look any different, but he kept quiet.

Once they were back in Alex's room, Walter, having slept for most of the day, found that he just couldn't drift off. *But he could have tried a bit harder*, Alex thought as he watched Walter jump up and down in delight.

'That's it!' Walter was saying. 'That's got to be it! The way we can get in and out of the churchyard. Why don't we go and try it out?'

Alex pointed out to him that it was far too late and that there was no way that his parents would let him leave the house when he should be going to bed.

'If you won't come with me,' said Walter huffily, 'I'll go by myself.'

And before Alex could think of a reason why he shouldn't, Walter lent against the bedroom wall and simply pushed right through it.

A minute later he appeared again. 'Don't worry about me, I'll be back before you wake in the morning.'

And then he vanished again.

Downstairs Alex's parents were watching television. Walter wasn't worried that they would see him. He was focusing with all of his might on not being seen. Still, he moved cautiously, floating through the house till he reached the utility room and found that the slab was again covered by carpet.

It was difficult for him to remember its exact position, and being a ghost he couldn't feel around for it. He picked a spot and tried a downward pushing motion, but nothing happened. He moved to a slightly different place and tried again, with no success. However, a third attempt – three times lucky was something he remembered his mother saying – was more successful, and he found himself sinking through the slab into the darkness of the steps below.

Usually he had no trouble seeing in the dark, but this was real darkness, no moonlight, no chink of light from above – just black. He sat on a step wishing that Alex was with him, holding the big torch that he kept in his bedroom.

Walter realised that he had no idea how long the tunnel was, or whether it was blocked anywhere along the way. All he could do was float along at a slow pace and hope for the best. He pictured himself as a bubble drifting in an obstacle course, hoping wildly that it wouldn't come up against something sharp that would burst it. Fortunately, he knew this last bit wasn't a risk to him; whatever he came up against, he could most likely pass through.

He started slowly down the steps, until he reached the bottom, then inched slowly along the tunnel through the deepest darkness he had ever known. On and on he floated, expecting with every moment to come up against the same invisible barrier that prevented him from entering the churchyard above ground. He must have come far enough now, he thought to himself. Down here, in the depths of the earth, there must not be a barrier. He hoped and hoped that he was right, and that the tunnel would prove to be the way in and out, meaning that Ned and Minnie could leave the churchyard so that all three of them might travel to the place that Minnie called Stonehenge.

Then he bumped into something, and his heart sank. He was just preparing to try and push his way through, when he realised that he'd reached another set of steps. This time they were heading upwards. Walter began to float vertically up, until he hit the tunnel roof at the top of the steps.

He paused. Could this be the slab that hid the entrance to the tunnel in the churchyard mausoleum? He was almost afraid to make the effort to push his way through. What if it wasn't the right place, and he ended up in someone else's house? The disappointment would be hard to bear. But he had to know, so with a huge effort he pushed himself upwards and through the slab.

CHAPTER SIXTEEN

Ned was feeling weepy again. He couldn't sleep. In fact, he had been sleepless for a long time. Too many memories were filling his head. e had been surprised to find that he could still remember the time when he was alive, even after three hundred years had gone by. He thought about his family and how as a boy he had often misbehaved. He thought about the kitchens where he had worked, and about the times when he hadn't been very kind to the people who worked with him. But most of all, he thought about Agnes.

Agnes was the girl he'd fallen in love with. They'd both worked in the big house, where she was a maid and he had been assistant cook at the time. Even after centuries had passed he could still picture her face and the way she'd looked at him. When they had both found that they had time off together, they would walk through the village and often sit in the churchyard.

Remembering Agnes made Ned both happy and sad. Happy because they'd spent time together and sad because their time had been short. A year or so after they'd met, Agnes and her parents had moved away from the village, so that her father could take up a job as head gardener at Northmead Castle. Soon after that, news came back that Agnes had drowned in the castle moat.

After that, it seemed to Ned that his whole world had fallen apart. He'd had plans to marry Agnes and had been saving money so that he could travel to the castle and inform her father of his intentions. Ned wanted to show him that he was serious about her, that he could offer her a good life with the money he'd saved.

But with Agnes gone, Ned became bad tempered. He took on the job of chief cook and made life hell for those who worked with him. He punished them if they made mistakes, and his rolling pin was more frequently used to deal out blows than it was to roll out dough. He had no time for anyone who fooled around in his kitchen or messed up his recipes, so when Walter had started dropping stones from the skylight into the dishes he'd baked, he'd been furious.

If he hadn't chased Walter, hoping to thrash him with the rolling pin, none of this would have happened. He wouldn't have followed him out onto the roof of the house, and he wouldn't have fallen when the tiles gave way.

Ned spent a lot of time with his thoughts, many of which started with the words 'If only...', and tonight he was sitting on the stone surround of the mausoleum feeling very sorry for himself.

It was then that he heard a voice close by, a voice he knew, whispering his name.

Walter floated out from the mausoleum and sat down by Ned, although not before first making sure that Ned wasn't holding his rolling pin.

'I'm sorry, Ned. I know I should have said it before but—'

Ned turned towards Walter.

'What does it matter now? It's all water under the bridge. I'm not angry anymore, just sad that I'll never get to be alive again and I'll never see Agnes again. That's what really pains me.'

'When Agnes moved away from the village, didn't she go to work at Northmead Castle?'

'Yes, she did.'

Walter told Ned about his visit to Northmead, and how he'd met up with several ghostly ladies.

Ned's eyes lit up. 'Do you think one of them might be Agnes?'

'I don't know, but there's a possibility.'

Ned looked sad again. 'Hardly matters now though, does it? I couldn't get to see her even if I knew she was there. There's no way I can leave the churchyard.'

'Actually, there is,' said Walter.

Ned eyed him sceptically.

'Think about it,' Walter said, grinning. 'Notice anything surprising?'

It took a moment for the penny to drop. 'Wait a minute,' Ned gasped. 'How did you get back into the churchyard?'

Minnie was sleeping fitfully. Normally sleep was something she could do very well as a ghost. Sometimes she'd sleep for months at a time, occasionally years at a time, and once she'd slept through a whole decade. It wasn't something she could keep track of herself, but Walter always seemed to know what year they were in, whenever she thought to ask him.

It was, of course, very quiet in the churchyard, and even more so in the tomb where she slept beside her coffin. When she had first become a ghost, she'd been surprised at how she never felt the cold. When she was alive, it had been something that troubled her. She'd always slept beneath a pile of rugs, but now a pile of leaves, which had been blown in under the broken base of the tomb, seemed to be all that she needed to make herself comfortable.

Since Ned had woken her, she hadn't been able to sleep properly. She kept thinking about whether they might find a way to move on, after all these years, if only it proved possible for them to leave the churchyard. Her school teacher's mind kept turning over ideas, briefly wondering if they might work, and then dropping them again as impossibilities.

Even if they were able to leave the churchyard, how

would they ever get to Stonehenge? How far was it? Could they float? Would someone have to take them? There were no satisfactory answers, and so Minnie just lay awake, staring into the gloom.

But it wasn't long before she heard a noise. It didn't seem like anything out of the ordinary at first, as the churchyard was seldom completely quiet at night. There were a couple of owls that hooted at each other, foxes that barked and badgers that snuffled about. As she listened, however, she realised that the sound came from none of these familiar companions. It was voices that she was hearing.

Voices in the churchyard at night were certainly unusual. There had been a lot of coming and going when Minnie first became a ghost. All sorts of rough-looking men tramped about in the darkness, carrying boxes and chests in and out of the mausoleum, shouting out to each other and not caring whether anyone heard them or not. They were smugglers, of course, cheating the system. Criminals, all of them, and Millie certainly hadn't approved of what they were doing.

And now there were voices again. Male voices. And they were coming closer.

Minnie pushed herself though the wall of her tomb and took a look. She saw two boys pause for a moment outside the mausoleum and look round. Then, satisfied that they weren't being watched, they pulled at the metal gate to the tomb and slipped inside. Minnie moved closer till she could see what they were doing. With a huge effort they pulled away the slab from the old smugglers' tunnel and disappeared down the steps.

At that moment she saw Walter and Ned and realised that they had also been watching what was taking place. Floating over to her, they whispered about the tunnel and how Walter had managed to get back into the churchyard. Then all three of them sat down to wait and see if Rafe and Frank came back again. Minnie and Ned were good at waiting. They'd waited for nearly three hundred years for something to happen that might allow them to leave the churchyard and move to the next stage of the afterlife. Now, at last, this could be their chance.

'I've often wondered what I'm doing here,' said Minnie. 'I can understand why you and Walter are here. It's because your lives were cut short and you had unfinished business that kept you from moving on, but I've spent decades puzzling over why *I'm* here. My life wasn't cut short. I was old when I passed on.'

Ned thought for a moment. 'Maybe you still have a job to do. Maybe your reason for staying behind is to show Walter and me what we need to do. You know about Stonehenge, and you seem fairly certain that it's the place we need to get to. That could well be your reason for remaining here.'

Walter wasn't quite so good at waiting and quickly grew bored. He thought that he'd sing a song to pass the time, and broke into a loud and ragged version of his favourite, 'Highway to Hell', complete with air guitar. Minnie and Ned were not impressed.

'If I have to spend eternity listening to you making that racket,' said Ned, 'I'll be looking for a way to kill myself all over again. SHUT UP!'

'All right,' Walter said. 'As you've obviously got no taste in music, let's follow them.'

It was one o'clock in the morning at the vicarage, and a noise from downstairs had woken everybody up. It was a creaking noise, and at first Mr Mitchell thought it was just the house settling. Then there were more noises. A louder creak. A muffled crash.

Mr Mitchell thought they were being burgled. He picked up a golf club that he kept in his bedroom and started to creep downstairs. His wife was behind him, whispering to him, telling him to be careful and not do anything stupid.

Phoebe and Alex were awake too, and followed, although their mum kept hissing at them to go back up. They looked in both of the downstairs rooms but soon it became clear that the noises were coming from the utility room. The carpet that covered the entranceway to the tunnel was shifting, and they could hear the slab beginning to lift. It was like something from a horror film. Everyone moved back except their dad, who approached the moving carpet.

Slowly it began to rise as someone, or something, pushed its way out of the tunnel. At that point Mr

Mitchell pulled back his golf club and swung it at whatever the carpet was hiding. There was a huge howl as the club connected with it, but fortunately it sounded like a human howl, and not something ghoulish.

Then their dad did something that Phoebe and Alex had never heard him do before. He swore at whoever it was who had howled. Still holding onto his golf club, he pulled the carpet towards him to reveal a very surprised and upset Rafe.

Fortunately, the golf club had only connected with Rafe's shoulder and not his head, although later Mr Mitchell said that he might have knocked some sense into Rafe if it had.

Then their dad allowed Rafe to emerge from the tunnel, quickly followed by Frank. Phoebe and Alex had never seen their dad so angry. His anger was monstrous. He swore again and told their mum to go and phone the police. He stood over them still holding the golf club in a threatening manner.

Rafe told their dad that he wasn't allowed to hit them with the golf club. He told him it was illegal. Then Mr Mitchell exploded again, telling Rafe that breaking into someone's house in the middle of the night was illegal too, and that he had every right to defend his property.

He went on and on at them, saying what he was going to do, how he'd be complaining to their parents and making sure the police took action against them.

For once in his life, Rafe decided it might be better to stay quiet, but Frank explained that they hadn't known where the tunnel went to, and that they certainly hadn't known that the tunnel's other entrance was in the old vicarage.

At that moment the doorbell rang, and two policemen arrived. They announced that they would take Rafe and Frank to the police station, something they recalled doing a few days earlier. They were none too pleased to be doing it again.

After the police had left, Mum made hot chocolate, and as they stood there drinking it, still staring at the tunnel entrance, it became apparent that something else was emerging, something greyish and see-through, but which quickly took on the form of a small boy.

'Walter!' Phoebe called out. He must have wanted their mum and dad to see him too, as his shape was as clear as Phoebe had ever seen it. Either that, or it was because now they *really* wanted to see him, or maybe a combination of both. He was very polite, telling them that he was sorry to disturb everyone further, but that he'd just had to find out if the tunnel was really an escape route from the churchyard.

Then there was more movement and grey matter around the tunnel entrance, and Walter, very politely again, said, 'May I introduce you to Minnie and Ned.'

CHAPTER SEVENTEEN

Whenever Mrs Mitchell had visitors to the old vicarage, she would offer them a cup of tea. This time too, after the initial shock of meeting two more ghostly figures, it was the first thing she thought of. Closely followed by 'How ridiculous'. Were there any books, she wondered, or anything online that told you how to behave when you found ghosts in your house? What on earth did you do with them? Should they report them? But who should they report them to?

She spoke out loud, 'What's to be done with them?'

Her husband had sat down in a chair – or more correctly, slumped. She didn't often see him lost for words, but right now he looked as bemused as she felt. Walter, Ned and Minnie hadn't moved. Mrs Mitchell thought they were probably just as unsure as to what to do as she was.

'They could have the spare bedroom, I suppose.'

Mr Mitchell looked at his wife with a look that asked, 'Have you gone stark raving mad?'

He sat up in his chair.

'Are you really proposing that we should open up

a B&B for ghosts? Well, they might be grateful for comfy beds to lie in, but surely there won't be much demand for breakfast.

'Haven't I got enough trouble,' he continued. 'The dead cause me plenty of problems in my work as an undertaker without them coming alive again. Please tell me that we're not about to receive any more visits from the spirit world tonight, I really would like to get some sleep. But before I do, I'm going to make sure nothing else comes through that trapdoor, either from this world or the next.'

With much grunting and groaning, Phoebe's dad managed to push a heavy chest of drawers till it covered the tunnel entrance.

'Now, does anyone want to use the bathroom before I go back to bed? I thought not. Don't suppose you three have any need for that sort of thing either.'

With that he went upstairs, leaving his wife to sort out the sleeping arrangements for their ghostly guests.

'We don't want to be a nuisance,' whispered Minnie. 'We can sleep anywhere.'

Phoebe's mum stared blankly at everyone. It was a situation that seemed to have drained her of the capacity to think straight. There were so many questions she ought to be asking, so many things they might be able to tell her, but not at that moment, not in the middle of the night with her brain so totally confused.

'Phoebe,' she said, 'please show our visitors to the

spare room. It seems the only option tonight. We can talk further in the morning.'

When Phoebe's mum woke next morning, after what seemed like a very short sleep, she tried to work out whether it had all been a dream. *Surely*, she thought, *we haven't welcomed three ghosts into our house.* She had always been a firm non-believer in ghosts, and suddenly that belief had been overturned.

Eventually she was forced to admit to herself that, no, it hadn't been a dream. It was all real. Ghosts were real, and three of them were staying in her home. The problem now was what was to be done with them.

Questions, questions, questions… Every moment that passed, she seemed to think of another one. Should she knock on the door and ask them how they'd slept? If they wanted anything? Should she have offered them separate rooms? After all, they weren't related in any way. What was socially acceptable in the spirit world? How long could they keep three ghosts in their house before someone found out? Should she insist that they return to the churchyard? What about Rafe? What did he know and who would he tell? It was all very worrying.

Her husband was still snoring, but she knew there'd be no chance of her getting back to sleep with all these thoughts scrambling around in her head. So she got up, went downstairs and made herself a coffee.

Soon afterwards Phoebe appeared and found

herself explaining to her mum all that she knew about the ghosts.

'I just don't understand, weren't you scared when you first saw them? Why didn't you tell us?' Mrs Mitchell asked.

'Would you have believed us if we had told you? I've heard you say to Dad that once you're dead you're dead, there's no coming back.'

Phoebe's mum thought for a moment. 'That's true, I suppose it's because of the work we do. As undertakers, dealing with the dead every day, we couldn't really allow ourselves to think otherwise. We would have gone crazy if we had done, but now it feels as if that craziness has caught up with us anyway. I'm worried, too, about how this will affect your dad. I don't think that last night he really took it all in.'

Phoebe explained to her mum how the ghosts needed to get to Stonehenge, then showed her the list that she'd started making when she hadn't been able to get to sleep herself. She had written across the top of the page, 'How do we get our ghosts to Stonehenge?'

Her mum appeared dazed as she took the list and looked at it.

So far Phoebe's ideas amounted to the following:

1. 'Floating. Ghosts can float, I've seen them do so. But can they float long distances? And how would they know which direction to travel in?
2. By train. Would they need tickets?

3. By car. Walter travelled in the car to Northmead Castle. All went OK apart from the awful smell on the way home.
4. By minibus. Could we ask Mr Khan to let us use the school minibus?
5. Could Mr Khan be persuaded to drive them to Stonehenge?
6. By ghostly coach and horses. (Check with Mr Khan.)

Mrs Mitchell read the list in a daze. She really had no idea what advice to offer. Phoebe offered to wake Alex, as they'd needed to talk with Walter, Ned and Minnie to get their ideas.

Outside the spare room door, Phoebe and Alex paused, wondering if they should knock before they went in. They decided it wasn't necessary and opened the door.

The room was noticeably cold. The curtains were closed tight, and a musty smell lingered in the room. Alex coughed. 'Is anyone awake?'

Gradually Walter began to materialise. He was yawning, still half asleep.

'We need to talk,' Phoebe spoke. 'We have to decide what's to be done with you.'

'We need to get to Stonehenge,' said Walter. 'It's just that there's been a complication.'

He admitted that he'd told Ned about the ghostly ladies of Northmead Castle. There was no way now that Ned would leave without knowing if one of them was Agnes, the girl he'd been in love with so many years ago.

'He wants to take her with him.'

'I can speak for myself.' Ned was awake. 'I've spent the last three hundred years without her, and now, if there's a chance of spending eternity in a more comfortable place than a gloomy churchyard, I'd like to share it with her.'

Phoebe and Alex looked at each other. This was an unexpected development.

Then Alex spoke, 'Ned, have you any idea as to how we can rescue her? How would we travel there, and how would we get into a castle that's locked for the night?'

'Well, I have been thinking, and there's a coach and horses that pass through the village now and then. It usually appears at midnight. I've watched them pass by as I've stood by the churchyard wall.'

Alex and Phoebe remembered what Mr Khan had said when they'd asked him about ghosts. He'd talked about rumours of a phantom coach and horses too.

'But how would they know that you wanted to get on board? You can hardly stand out there by the village bus stop and stick your arm out.'

'Ah, but I've seen them stop outside this house. I think it must have been a funeral hearse taking away the dead.'

Just then they all heard a knock on the front door that reverberated through the house. This was followed by several knocks and a shout from Mrs Mitchell, telling whoever it was not to be so impatient.

Next they heard raised voices, and one of them was Rafe's. He was demanding that he be let in as he had a photographer with him from the newspaper. They could hear the photographer speaking more politely, but it was obvious that Mrs Mitchell was holding on to the door to stop them entering.

'Look,' pleaded Rafe, in a whiny voice, 'I promise you that any money we make from photographing these ghosts will go straight to charity.'

They heard their mum's answer. 'I don't care what you promise, and for a start I don't believe any of it, but you are not coming into this house. There are no ghosts here, they've returned to the churchyard.'

Then they heard the photographer again, 'So there *are* ghosts. You've seen them? I wasn't sure about what this lad old me, but I'm more inclined to believe you.'

Mrs Mitchell ignored him, managing to push the door shut, but not before everyone heard the photographer call out, 'I won't be giving up!'

CHAPTER EIGHTEEN

Alex and Phoebe both knew that it would be a monumental task to persuade their parents to do what needed to be done next. How could they explain that they needed to take two journeys, the first to Northmead Castle to see if Ned could find Agnes, and the second much longer journey to Stonehenge in the hope that the ghosts could move on to the next stage of their travels in the afterlife.

They talked and talked, both by themselves and then with Walter, Ned and Minnie. The assorted ladies at Northmead Castle had told Walter that they couldn't leave the castle. Presumably there was some invisible force stopping them, something similar to the one that surrounded the village churchyard. So how would they overcome that and rescue Agnes?

Phoebe felt that her mum and dad would never agree to a rescue mission. They were still coming to terms with having three ghosts staying in their house. The prospect of a fourth surely wouldn't go down well.

Phoebe felt that, very soon, her parents would insist that the ghosts return to the churchyard. Then there was the problem of Rafe too. He wouldn't give up; they knew him too well. Something would need to be done about him very soon.

'Tell us more about the coach and horses, please, Ned,' said Alex.

'Well, it's pretty ghastly. The coach driver is certainly headless, and it looks to me as if he keeps his head in a bag on the seat alongside him.'

Phoebe's face showed an expression of disgust. However, she knew that, if they ever needed something to distract Rafe, telling him about this particular ghost would be perfect. He would no doubt find the idea of a ghostly severed head fascinating.

'It seems like the coach is made of bones rather than wood, with a skull fixed at each corner of the roof. I remember my father telling me about it when I was a boy. He loved to frighten me by saying that, if I misbehaved, he'd stop the coach and throw me on board. That really used to make me shiver. He used to tell me that it made its way to the castle and back each night, but I never saw it. I was too scared to look for it.'

Walter, who had been quiet for a while, suddenly jumped up and called out, 'I'm up for it. It might be the real highway to hell! Shall we do it tonight?'

'I'd better go along too,' said Minnie. 'If we do find poor Agnes, she'll be terrified. Hopefully I can try to calm her fears.'

Phoebe and Alex looked at each other. 'Now all we

have to do,' said Phoebe, 'is to explain to our parents that we need to leave the house around midnight and travel to the castle in a phantom coach and horses with a headless driver… Easy!'

'I don't think you'll need to do all that,' said Ned. 'I don't think the living can travel in a ghostly coach. Maybe it would work if we could make you honorary ghosts for the night, but there's no way we can do that. You'll have to get there by some other means.'

Phoebe could think of only one possibility. Their dad would have to drive them there in his car – but could they persuade him to do that?

On their way downstairs, Phoebe and Alex looked out at the street. On the opposite side they saw Rafe along with the reporter who had tried to push his way through their front door. They had now been joined by a camera crew who had set up a camera on a tripod and were pointing it towards the house. A microphone was being held up to one of their neighbours, who happened to be out on the street. Doubtless they were asking her about what she knew of ghostly happenings at the funeral parlour.

They found their dad in an angry mood. He hated the unwanted attention that his ghostly visitors had brought him. All his life he had been happy – or as reasonably happy as someone with SAD could be – just leading a quiet life. It wasn't the job he'd dreamed of when he was at school. He'd passed his exams and had wanted to go to university, but the funeral business had been in the family for many generations. He'd accepted that he'd join the family business in the end, and now all he wanted was for things to get back to normal.

His first reaction when Phoebe outlined their plans for the ghosts was an angry 'No!' He jumped out of his seat and started pacing around the room.

'This is crazy!' he said. 'We are meddling with the unknown, the unexplained, the afterlife, all things that we have no right to be meddling with. They must go back to the churchyard, and you must forget all this has happened.'

Mrs Mitchell looked thoughtful. 'Perhaps you should consider, Robert, that these spirits may have touched our lives in this way because they really do need our help. Now I know nothing about ghosts, but it seems as if they do still have human feelings. They still feel the emotions they felt when they were alive, and for us to ignore them and to banish them again just doesn't seem right. We've always believed in assisting people when we can, and this is just a different sort of help to the help we usually give.'

And so it went on, backwards and forwards, their parents seemingly engaged in a game of word tennis, where one served up an argument only to have it lobbed back by the other.

Phoebe and Alex were desperate that the ghosts should be helped to move on to the next stage of their afterlife, but nothing they said seemed to impress their dad.

It took the best part of three hours before something that Mrs Mitchell said seemed to make a bit of a difference. She reminded her husband how he'd often complained that his life had been ordinary, that he hadn't done anything different or exciting. It was a mundane life, he often said, but he'd made the best of it.

'Now's your chance,' she told him. 'Make a difference.'

'There's one other thing,' said Alex. 'Phoebe and I have asked Walter lots of questions about his life as a child. He told us about the smuggling that went on in the village, and we told him how sad and disappointed you are that our ancestors were criminals.'

'I am. It upsets me to think about it.'

'But you don't know the full story. Walter told us that the smugglers threatened to kill his father if they didn't let them use their cellars to store their goods. Everyone was terrified of them. They meant what they said. Then after Walter died and the smuggling ring was broken up, no one believed they were innocent and they were put in prison. So it wasn't their fault, Dad.'

He slumped down in a chair and stared at the floor. Five minutes passed till he spoke. 'Thank you for telling us that,' he said to Walter. 'It's as if the black cloud hanging over our family for all these years has finally been lifted.'

He turned to look at Phoebe and Alex. 'Now, if we do help the ghosts, and it's still a big "if", how do you propose going about it?'

After Phoebe and Alex had explained their plan, their dad nodded seriously, said that he'd do it, but that it was still against his better judgement. Phoebe and Alex high-fived. With their dad, that was about as enthusiastic a 'yes' as you got.

CHAPTER NINETEEN

During the evening a bank of cloud had brought rain to the village, quite a lot of rain, but by 11pm the clouds had moved on and the night was clear. There had been talk about waiting for better weather, but in the end Phoebe's dad declared that there was no time like the present, and that he wanted to get it over with.

Everyone was pleased to see that the rain had driven off the reporter and his camera crew, but they decided not to take any chances and went out the back way to find the car. How surreal it all seemed, taking a drive in the dark with three phantom figures in the back of the car alongside Alex and Phoebe.

Briefly Mrs Mitchell wondered if their ghostly companions should be wearing seat belts, but she quickly dismissed the idea.

Ned and Minnie sat very still and hardly said a word. It was almost three hundred years since Ned had said goodbye to Agnes, when she had left the house where he was cook and moved to the castle with her family.

Would she still recognise him after all these years? And that was if she was even there in the first place. And what if there was another ghost in the castle who had become her companion, and if so, would she want to know him? All these thoughts bothered him as they sped through the dark.

Halfway to the castle, Walter could no longer contain himself. '*We're on the highway to hell!*' he called out, in a sinister-sounding crackle of a voice.

Mr Mitchell started joining in too. Phoebe and Alex were amazed, but at the same time pleased to see him happy. It was a rare thing. 'How do you know this song, Dad?' Pheobe asked.

'I haven't always been the age I am now, despite what you may think. This was a popular song when I was a teenager. My mates and I would sing it as we were driving along. AC/DC, Led Zeppelin, Black Sabbath, we listened to them all. The vinyl albums are in the attic somewhere. Maybe I should get them down and listen to them again.'

'I wish you still had your rolling pin,' whispered Minnie to Ned. 'I'd happily give Walter a bop if he sings that dreadful song one more time.'

There was very little traffic at that time of night, and they reached the castle quite quickly. Some castles have spotlights that pick out particular features at night, but Northmead was shrouded in darkness. The castle entrance loomed above them, with only the light from a quarter moon to break up the gloom. All in all, it didn't look very hopeful that they might find a way into the castle, if one even existed at all.

Everyone got out of the car. Phoebe went to open the door for the ghosts but realised, of course, that they had no need of open doors. They'd simply pushed their way out and were hovering close by.

There was a high wall around the castle, and at one point an entranceway. Two heavy wrought iron gates stopped anyone getting through, although it was possible to peer through the bars and see what was happening in the castle courtyard. If the humans were to follow the ghosts into the castle, the gates looked like their best hope. Maybe they could squeeze between the bars.

Just at that moment, they saw and heard another car approaching. There was no way to identify who was in the vehicle, and the headlights on full beam meant that everyone was temporarily blinded. It pulled up behind Mr Mitchell's car, and the engine was turned off. When the doors opened, everyone realised that they hadn't given Rafe and his reporter friend the slip after all.

'So, what's happening here?' asked Rafe. 'Why didn't we get an invitation to this party? I guess we'll just have to gatecrash it, Dave.'

While he spoke, Dave set up his camera for night scenes. He took several quick shots of the gate and yelled out in shock when he found three ghostly figures showing up in the photographs.

At that moment, Phoebe became conscious of another noise: a whooshing noise from the lane behind them and the thunderous sound of hooves on stone. It was moments after midnight, and as everyone turned around to see what was approaching, Phoebe could hear the crack of a whip and see the outline of a hearse-like coach and horses. She saw the headless coachman tugging on the reins to bring the demonic manifestation to a halt a short way away from them.

It was everything that Ned had described. Two skeletal stallions shaking their long black manes, snorting and pawing the ground. The coachman reached down and then held aloft his head. His eyes were blazing, and at that point Phoebe realised that she'd made a mistake. She should have warned her parents. They'd coped incredibly well with the ghostly gang up to that point, but a headless coachman and a coach of skulls and bones was way too much for either of them. To his credit Phoebe's dad pushed both Phoebe and her mum behind him and showed great courage, facing up to something that looked as if it had indeed just driven along a highway from hell.

Rafe, on the other hand, after the initial shock had passed, was jumping up and down in sheer delight. 'Wow,' they heard him say, 'Wow, wow, wow!' And then to Dave, 'Get pictures, quick.'

Dave, however, had put some distance between himself and the coach and horses, and any pictures he took would suffer from a bad case of camera shake. The guy was trembling uncontrollably.

Next they saw that Ned, Minnie and Walter were in the coach. They heard the crack of a whip, and the horses began pulling their dreadful vehicle towards the castle gates. Phoebe, Alex and her parents jumped to one side as the horses thundered towards them. Then the coachman, coach and horses passed straight through the gates and into the castle courtyard.

'Well, that's useless,' Rafe called out. 'How are we supposed to get through?'

He gazed between the bars at the gloomy courtyard for a moment, and then, hit by an idea, he ran back to Dave's car and took out a carrier bag. 'You'd better not let me down this time.' They heard him say as he ran back to the gates.

'What's he got in that bag?' Alex asked Phoebe.

'I've got a horrible suspicion I know what it is,' she answered.

Ralph stuck his hand inside the bag and withdrew the hand of glory that he'd found in the village churchyard (although a better description might have been 'bones of glory'). He held them against the lock on the gate. 'Open,' he yelled. 'Open up.'

Alex smiled at Phoebe. 'Fat chance of that happening.'

Rafe called out again, twisting and turning the bones.

Nothing happened for a minute, but then it was as

if the bony fingers had tuned into some spectral transmission: slowly, very slowly, and creakily, the gates began to swing open.

'I just don't believe this,' Phoebe said.

No one was more surprised than Rafe. 'It works, it actually works! It opens locked gates.' Then slipping the hand back into the bag, he ran through to the courtyard.

'Quick,' Alex shouted to Phoebe, 'before the gates close again!'

Phoebe hesitated for a moment and then raced after Alex. Their dad grabbed hold of his wife's hand, 'We can't let them go on their own.'

Before the gates closed fully, their parents and Dave had squeezed through and were in the castle courtyard.

As the gates swung shut behind them, with an ominous creak, Mrs Mitchell turned to her husband. 'Did you remember to lock the car, dear?' she asked.

Inside the great hall of the castle, Walter, Minnie and Ned were not having much success. They floated in the darkness, looking all around and listening for any noise or movement that might indicate the presence of other ghosts.

'How did you find them last time?' Ned asked Walter.

'I just seemed to sense someone was watching me, and then I started talking to a green lady.'

Ned pressed on, 'Do you remember anything about her?'

'She liked to sing. She sang with a ghostly choir of red, grey and white ladies.'

'Why don't you sing something now. That might let them know that we're here.'

'Do you think that's wise?' whispered Minnie. 'He only knows one song, if you can even call it a song.'

'Try it, all the same,' said Ned, 'We're desperate.'

'Not that desperate,' Minnie answered. 'Let's just wait—'

'WE'RE ON THE HIGHWAY TO HELL, WE'RE ON THE HIGHWAY TO HELL...'

'Don't you know any more of the song? It's so awful.'

It may have been awful, but it seemed to get results. They were suddenly aware of a swishing noise from the balcony where Walter had previously seen the ghostly ladies. Then they heard a rasping voice.

'It's that cute boy again, sisters, but he's singing that dreadful song.'

As before, Walter heard a chorus of disapproval:

'No, no, no!'

'That's far too loud.'

'It's not just loud, it's hurting my ears.'

'Make him stop.'

'Never heard anything like it.'

'Send him away.'

By now they could all see that the voices belonged to a colourful row of ghostly ladies, most of whom had their hands pressed to their ears.

'Maybe he's come back to join our choir, and look, if I'm not mistaken he's brought with him two companions. Maybe they sing too.'

Ned had no patience for this chatter. He was on a mission. If you've ever wondered whether a ghost can shout, instead of just wandering around sighing and whispering, then you should have heard Ned. He put all the anger and frustration of his lonely existence for the past three hundred years into a mournful, heart-breaking howl that echoed around the Great Hall:

'AGNES!'

The ghostly ladies clapped their hands back over their ears till the noise subsided, and then all that could be heard were their disapproving voices.

'I haven't heard anyone make a noise like that since my husband's stallion trod on his foot.'

'Sounded like the voice of doom!'

'It's done something to my ears. I can't hear anything now.'

'Worse than the song that wretched boy sings.'

'Don't let him do it again.'

After the excited voices calmed down, Walter asked, 'Is anyone here called Agnes?'

The voices again:

'I'm Esther.'

'Mary.'

'Harriet.'

'Ada.'

'Henrietta.'

'Eliza.'

A red-tinged lady then spoke up. 'Sisters, don't you remember, there was someone called Agnes, two or maybe three hundred years back. She wouldn't stop weeping, on and on and on, day and night, about never seeing her man again. Drove us all mad! We couldn't rest.'

'What happened to her?' Ned called out.

The ladies looked at each other. They seemed reluctant to speak. Finally, after what seemed an eternity to Ned, the red lady spoke again in a sorrowful voice. 'We sent her away. Told her to go to another part of the castle, well away from us, somewhere we couldn't hear her weeping.'

They heard another voice. 'We did tell her to come back once she'd cheered up a bit. But she didn't, and we haven't seen her since.'

There was another desperate wail from Ned as he heard the news.

Minnie took charge. 'We need to search for her, all of us. Surely she must still be here somewhere.'

Ghosts, of course, don't set off security alarms, but humans do.

Before they had taken many steps across the castle courtyard there was the shrieking noise of an alarm. It was an ear-splitting sound that rose and fell in an almighty racket that sent everyone's hands to their ears. The ghostly ladies were beside themselves, barely having recovered from the racket of Walter and Ned.

Phoebe mouthed at Alex, 'What do we do now?'

Rafe and Dave looked at each other and then began to search for somewhere to hide, while Alex and Phoebe's parents looked devastated. In their hurry to pass through the castle gates no one had considered that they would probably be alarmed. Her parents had never been on the wrong side of the law till now, and Phoebe could see that they were panic-stricken. How would they be able to explain their presence in the castle?

In what seemed like a very short period of time, they saw the lights of a car approaching on the road outside, and a flashing blue light which indicated that the police had arrived. What possible excuse could there be for their midnight trespassing?

CHAPTER TWENTY

If there had been any ghosthunters in the rooms and passages of Northmead Castle that night, they would have been astonished at what they saw. Maybe there's a noun for a group of ghosts – a gaggle of ghosts, a flotilla of ghosts, a flurry of ghosts. Maybe ghosthunters have coined a phrase already. Whatever it is, they would have seen one that night.

First Walter came floating along at top speed, closely followed by Ned. Next came Minnie, leading a variety of red, grey and white ladies who were all talking excitedly.

'Poor Agnes, what have we done?'

'Oh, Agnes, will you ever forgive us?'

'You were so sad, and we were so selfish.'

'Let's listen, maybe we'll hear her.'

'Oh, Agnes.'

Walter stopped abruptly, only to find that his ghostly companions couldn't apply the brakes as easily. They all coalesced into one shapeless ghostly blob.

'Do you ladies have any idea where she might have gone?' Walter asked, once he had squirmed out of the pileup.

The ladies gradually returned to their own shapes and started shaking their heads. Then the green-tinged lady said, 'Maybe she went back to her bedroom. I have heard talk about a room of tears where visitors have said they've heard weeping.'

Ned grew excited. 'Where's that? Take me there quickly!'

They found stairs to the upper levels of the castle and quickly climbed them. They then passed a number of empty rooms until the ghostly ladies stopped by a door and began chattering all at once.

'Was this Agnes' bedroom?' Ned asked.

'We're quite sure it was,' said Harriet.

Ned leant against the door then slowly eased his way through the wood and into the darkened room beyond.

'Agnes!' he called.

There was no sound of weeping and no answering call. The room was empty.

Ned sank to the floor in despair. How many more times could he bear to have his hopes dashed like this?

Just then Walter appeared in the room.

'The ladies have been saying that if she isn't in her room, you should try the castle library. Apparently that was her happy place, and she spent a long time reading there. That's where they think she could be.'

Ned gave another most unghostly cry before

pushing his way through the door, closely followed by Walter.

'Where's the library?' he pleaded.

'Follow us,' said Harriet, but Ned was far too impatient to follow anyone. He floated off at a ridiculously fast speed for a ghost, so fast that he was in danger of leaving parts of himself behind.

'Go down the stairs,' he heard a voice call out behind him. 'It's the room on the right.'

Again Ned floated down the stairs as if they were a slippery slide, pulled himself together at the bottom, and pushed his way through the library door.

He heard the weeping as soon as he entered the room. It was a sound that would have broken his heart if he'd still had a heart to break. Even so, it dragged up every last bit of his leftover human feelings of pity until he thought that they would overwhelm him.

'Agnes,' he called, 'is that really you?'

The sobbing stopped and he heard a whisper. 'Ned, it can't be. You're not really here.'

A shadow detached itself from a window seat, and Ned could see Agnes at last. Although it was three hundred long, long years since he'd last seen her, he felt the love that he had for her burst out of him.

'Agnes, it is, it's me, I've come for you.'

Walter, who had entered the room behind Ned, heard Agnes reply through tears, but tears of happiness this time. 'Oh, Ned, I can't believe it. I've been so very unhappy.'

Then the library was full of ghosts all talking and laughing at the same time, drowning out the hissing noises that must surely have been Ned and Agnes kissing.

Back at the castle entrance, the police were having a hard time making any sense out of what Mr and Mrs Mitchell were telling them. They were unable to get into the courtyard, and all conversation took place with the gate between them.

The first policeman who approached was actually someone they knew, someone who had often popped into the undertaker's office on routine police enquiries. He shone his torch into their faces, and seemed shocked at what he saw.

'Good evening, sir, madam, ah, it's Mr Mitchell, I see, and Mrs Mitchell. I wonder if you'd mind telling us what you're doing here. You realise, I'm sure, that you are trespassing on private property?'

Mr Mitchell looked as if he wished the ground would open up and swallow him. There didn't seem any possible logical reason for their presence. A number of explanations occurred to him, but all of them were totally ridiculous:

'We've just driven three ghosts to the castle so that they can look for several more.'

'We are a taxi service for those who didn't quite make it to the afterlife.'

'We're an online service called Ghosts Reunited.'

Alex looked at Phoebe. What on earth could their

dad say?

'It's a very long story, I'm afraid,' he finally replied, 'and you certainly won't believe it. Can I ask you, do you believe in ghosts?'

'Mr Mitchell,' the police officer replied, 'it is I who should be asking the questions. Please explain yourself.'

Their dad did his best to be truthful, as he always did, but they could all see the incredulous look spreading across the policeman's face.

'Mr Mitchell, I know that you deal with the dead on a daily basis, but I thought when they came to you, they stayed dead. Are you suggesting that some of them don't?'

Mr Mitchell looked at the floor, at his wife, at the night sky, anywhere but the policeman in front of him. He couldn't think what to say so he stayed silent.

'Mr Mitchell,' said the policeman, 'Have you been drinking?'

'I certainly have not.'

'I think I believe you, but I do need to make certain. In a moment, when the warden arrives to open the gates, I'll ask you to step across to the police car, please, and we'll get you to blow into a bag.'

This was total mega embarrassment for Alex and Phoebe's dad, as he waited to be escorted from the courtyard, but just at that moment, the castle warden arrived. He'd been phoned by the police when they knew that there had been a break in.

Another policeman started talking to him and asked

how the intruders might have got through a locked gate.

Phoebe and Alex looked at each other. How would he explain that one?

'Actually,' the warden said, 'I think I know what happened. The gate has a fault. It's been opening and closing at random for a couple of days now. I thought I'd fixed it, but obviously not. It opens when pressure is applied at a certain point. Unfortunately, I couldn't get a locksmith to look at it till tomorrow.'

'So it wasn't Rafe's hand of glory after all,' whispered Alex. 'He will be disappointed.'

Just then there was a commotion in the courtyard. Rafe and Dave had broken cover and Dave was struggling with his camera as shadowy figure after shadowy figure emerged from the castle keep and assembled in the courtyard. They became a blur of green, grey, red and white ladies, with Ned somewhere in the middle of them all, and Minnie with Walter looking on.

And then there was Dave taking photo after photo. He couldn't believe his luck. It would be a world-class exclusive in the papers the next day.

It took the police a while to corral Rafe and Dave, with Dave snapping away the whole time. However, once the trespassers had been dragged out of the gates, the police could get no more sense out of them than they could from the Mitchells. It was obvious that they couldn't see the ghosts at all. Alex heard one of them say to his colleague, 'I've no idea how we're going to explain this in the police report.'

Then everyone was leaving. No one would be prosecuted as there was no damage done and the owner of the castle was partly to blame for not sorting out their faulty gate. The police were satisfied that Mr Mitchell hadn't been drinking, and as soon as the gates closed behind them, they were back in their car and on their way.

The castle warden was facing a similar problem regarding the report of the incident that he would have to submit.

'Look,' he started, 'can someone give me an explanation as to what you're doing here?'

Mr Mitchell tried once more. He told the truth, but the truth was so incredible that the warden declared that he didn't believe a word of it.

'I have been warden here for over twenty years, and I tell you for a fact, there are no ghosts haunting this castle.'

Just as he spoke, Ned began to lead his group of ghosts towards the coach and horses, which he was hoping would allow them to leave the castle. They passed behind the warden's back as he was speaking. If the warden had turned around, would he have seen them? Who knows. Alex and Phoebe remembered how Walter had said that ghosts were only visible to those people with an open mind, to those who *wanted* to see ghosts, and even then, only if the ghosts themselves wanted to be seen.

'Mr Mitchell,' the warden said, 'you do not seem like a mad person to me, but what you are saying is madness. Would you all please leave the castle? I would like to get some rest myself tonight, even though I shall now need to stay here till the locksmith arrives in the morning.'

Rafe and Dave couldn't control their excitement. The photos that Dave had taken would be the ultimate proof that ghosts existed. There could be both money and fame for them. Dave was already thinking of how he might auction his photos to the highest bidder. All the newspapers would want them, he was sure of that. Once they'd worked out that there was no way they could have been Photoshopped, they'd pay plenty.

Alex, Phoebe and their parents all watched Rafe and Dave speed off in Dave's car.

'Once that photo gets in the papers,' said Mr Mitchell, 'we will have the world's press camped out on our doorstep, all hoping to get photos of their own. I just don't know how we're going to handle this.'

Just at that moment they heard a clatter of hooves and snorting noises as the ghostly horses and coach swept past them all, through the castle gateway, till it came to a halt once more in the courtyard beyond the gates.

The group of ghosts all started speaking at once...

'Where are we going?'

'What do we do now?'

'I don't think I want to leave this castle.'

'It's been our home for more than three hundred years.'

They all turned to Ned, who was trying to explain their plan, as one by one they floated out of the coach.

Phoebe and Alex's parents looked like they'd managed to convince themselves that the whole ghostly mess had been nothing more than a bad dream, and were now being forced to accept the truth all over again. Their mother sighed and said, 'I suppose we'd better take everyone home with us, till we can sort out how to get them to Stonehenge.'

She turned to her husband. 'Can we get ten ghosts plus Phoebe and Alex in the back of our car?'

Walter had been listening and replied, 'It will be fine if I can get everyone to shrink a little.'

He explained what was needed, gleefully warning that any shrinking would be accompanied by loud farting noises.

'It really is the only way,' said Walter. 'Look, I'll show you.' And with that he wrapped his arms around himself, squeezed in his cheeks and blew out a rude noise which had the effect of making him shrink to a third of his normal size.

'Oh no,' said Minnie, 'I can't do that, I was brought up too well. My parents would get very upset if I ever did that within their earshot.'

By now the others had all begun to copy Walter's example. Ned and Agnes were holding tight to each other, while the ladies all held hands and seemed to be attempting some sort of synchronised shrinking.

Minnie was pacing up and down, wrestling with her conscience, till finally she admitted defeat and, with a supreme effort, and a huge farting sound, she shrank to a third of her size. Alex felt sure that he could see a red tinge to her face, where she was blushing from embarrassment.

Then everyone squeezed into the car where, surrounded by cold ghostly shapes, Phoebe and Alex began to feel very chilly indeed.

Mrs Mitchell had all kinds of concerns as they drove back. Would the ghosts all be happy staying together in the spare room, or should she offer Ned and Agnes Phoebe's room? How long would they have to stay with them, and how would they get away if the house was surrounded by newspaper reporters?

Just then her thoughts were interrupted as a dreadful and familiar stink spread through the car. 'Stop the car, Dad,' yelled Phoebe. 'Quick!'

The car stopped, doors opened and everyone jumped out. They stood breathing in great lungfuls of fresh air. There was no doubt again that Walter was the cause of this disruption, once again bringing the odour of history far too close for comfort.

'Oh, Walter,' Phoebe said disapprovingly. 'This has got to stop.'

CHAPTER TWENTY-ONE

Like most people, when you're busy in the bathroom, you probably like to be alone. Mrs Mitchell was no different. She'd had very little sleep since they'd returned from the castle and was hoping a shower might bring her back to life.

Also like most people, when preparing for a shower, Mrs Mitchell preferred not to find any company in the bathroom. But as she stared into the mirror, she discovered a reddish glow in the shape of a human figure standing behind her.

'Look,' she said, 'you can go where you like in the house, but please stay out of the bathroom when it is being used.'

'I'm so sorry,' came the reply. 'I was just curious. That toilet paper looks so soft and gentle. We had to make do with much rougher stuff. And it's so warm here. You'd never believe how cold it could be taking a wash in the castle.

'And where's your cesspit?' the ghostly voice continued. 'We had an awfully smelly cesspit in the castle. They used to make the prisoners clean it out. I felt so sorry for them!'

Mr Mitchell, meanwhile, was downstairs feeding the dog when he realised that he wasn't alone. The dog suddenly stopped bolting his food and backed away into a corner. He looked terrified.

Something insubstantial, but with an unmissably green tinge, was forming in the kitchen. As it took on human form it became clearer, and Mr Mitchell recognised the green lady from Northmead Castle. She floated across the room till she was very close to him, and he heard a whisper of a voice. 'Thank you so much for rescuing us,' she said.

At that moment he felt a cold damp touch on his cheek and realised that he had been kissed by a ghost.

Mrs Mitchell arrived in the kitchen to find him looking terribly flustered, but by that time the green lady had vanished. He smiled to himself, wondering if he ought to tell his wife what had happened.

Walter was up and about too. Alex was still sleeping, but when he had woken briefly, disturbed by his mum slamming the bathroom door, Walter had seized his chance to ask him to turn on his favourite AC/DC playlist.

But even positioned between the headphones, Walter could hear the commotion from the road outside. He floated across to the window and looked down.

Phoebe and her parents had also heard the disturbance, and were already peering out of the window at the street. Several reporters with cameras had camped out on the other side of the road. Presumably Rafe's reporter friend Dave had spread the word about the photos he'd taken at the castle. As they watched, one person from the huddle left the group and crossed the street. Next thing they heard was a vigorous knocking on the front door.

'Don't answer it,' warned Mrs Mitchell.

'Nonsense,' said her husband. 'Not only am I going to answer it, I'm going to tell these people just where they can go.'

Next thing everyone heard was Mr Mitchell's raised voice doing just that, but his appearance at the door provoked a flurry of camera activity from across the street, and he quickly slammed it shut again.

'We need to sort this problem out, and soon,' Phoebe heard him mutter to her mum.

As the day went on, more and more reporters joined the crowd, blocking access to houses and disturbing life in the village.

Even when evening came, some of them stayed put, wrapped in blankets and determined to get the scoop. There had been several more knocks on the door, but they'd all been ignored.

Family and ghosts went to sleep that night with the problem still unresolved. They were woken after midnight by a noise from downstairs.

The heavy chest of drawers still covered the entrance to the tunnel, but it was obvious that Rafe must have shown his reporter friends how to find their way through, and they were now attempting to lift the slab. Phoebe's dad stood guard with his golf club again, but he needn't have worried. The chest was doing its job, and nobody could shift it.

After that he didn't get much sleep, and by the time morning came he had changed his mind. There was no way now that he would be travelling to Stonehenge with a car full of ghosts, chased by a pack of journalist and amateur ghost hunters. No way indeed.

Rafe and his reporter friend Dave had done their work well. Photographs showing several ghosts leaving Northmead Castle were published in several of the national newspapers. They were accompanied by statements from experts in photography who stated that the photos were real and not Photoshopped.

Alex and Phoebe were eating their breakfast when they discovered that the photos had also caught the attention of *Good Morning Britain*, where a panel of experts had been called upon to give their opinion.

Several of their ghostly guests had drifted downstairs and were amazed to see themselves on the TV screen. The picture then changed to the road outside, where a huge throng of reporters and camera folk were gathered.

The TV also showed Northmead Castle, where there were even more reporters hanging around the entrance, trying to obtain comments from anyone entering.

'Whatever anyone does this morning,' warned Mr Mitchell, 'don't answer the door. I have a funeral today, and they had better not block me in.'

As Mr Mitchell left the house, reporters swarmed round him shouting out questions, but he stayed tight-lipped. He pushed his way through them and out to his office in the yard.

Phoebe looked at Alex. 'How are we going to get our ghosts out of here and off on their journey to Stonehenge?'

'I think I may have an idea,' Alex said. 'Those reporters and camera people won't stop the hearse leaving for a funeral, particularly if there's a coffin in the back. If the ghosts can hide in an empty coffin, that could be the way out.'

As he explained, Phoebe's eyes lit up and she clapped her hands. 'Yes,' she said, jumping up. 'That could be it!'

Ned, who had been listening, agreed. 'It sounds like a good plan to me.'

The ghosts were all enjoying watching television. They had so many questions about the things they saw that Phoebe and Alex spent most of the next hour trying to answer them. Ned thought he might like to try driving a car, and Minnie thought that flying in a plane would be incredibly exciting.

The singing ladies from the castle were particularly fascinated by the adverts on TV, and all the wonderful things that would have made their lives so much easier if they'd been around in their day.

Later in the day the family gathered together in the living room: Phoebe and Alex, their mum and dad, and a variety of ghosts. Only Walter was missing, preferring to remain in Alex's room and listen to his music.

Minnie looked glum. 'I'm so sad that we have to leave. To be honest, here in your lovely house is the first time I've really felt warm in three hundred years. Couldn't we just stay a bit longer?'

Phoebe and Alex looked at each other, and then at their mum. She looked sad, but their dad looked as if he was about to explode.

Before he could say anything, Ned spoke up. 'I'd like to stay too. I've only just found Agnes again after all this time, and I'm frightened that I might lose her again if we move to a different place.'

'And we'd like to stay as well,' one of the grey ladies said. 'It's so different to being in that cold castle. You've no idea how many times we've longed for warmth, for a fire that we could be close to, and to feel the heat within us once more.'

Alex thought that Walter would probably want to

stay too. He'd left him upstairs compiling a playlist of his favourite heavy metal songs.

The green lady spoke next. 'We've loved seeing all the clothes that everyone wears these days, and watching television. I want to know what happens next in *Coronation Street*!'

There was a sound of sheer exasperation from Phoebe and Alex's dad. 'Oh, this is ridiculous!' he said. 'But you might all get your wish. There's no way we can get you out of here with all these reporters swarming everywhere. They'll see us and they'll chase us. It will be far too dangerous.'

'We've thought of how it could be done,' Alex said. He turned to the ghosts. 'If you lot decide you still want to give it a try, that is.'

He briefly outlined the plan.

'I'm sorry,' their dad said, once Alex had finished. 'It's far too risky, even if you could get your friends here to agree to it.' And with that he walked out the room.

Phoebe turned to her mum. 'What will happen to the ghosts?' she asked.

'I don't know yet,' Mrs Mitchell said with a sigh. 'I'll talk to your dad and see what he's got in mind. Meanwhile they can stay here for the moment.'

CHAPTER TWENTY-TWO

GHOSTS ALIVE!

It has come to our attention that the village of Darvale in Sussex may just be the most haunted village in England.

A series of photographs taken at the nearby Northmead Castle seems to show a number of ghostly figures in and around the village, and according to our journalist who took the shot, three further ghosts have been seen in the village churchyard. Experts have assured us that the photograph is genuine, and it seems that the world's press are now camped on the pavement outside the village funeral parlour, where the ghosts are said to be residing.

All attempts to interview anyone at the property have been rebuffed, and nothing has been seen of the ghosts since their trip back from the castle over a week ago. The local police have informed us that they do not consider this a police matter and that they can't get involved.

No one is prepared to issue a search warrant so that this strange situation can be properly investigated.

Funerals are still taking place, and these are being allowed to pass through the throng of reporters outside the property.

It does seem, however, that the chance of witnessing not one, but several ghosts in the same location, is drawing amateur ghosthunters to the village alongside the press.

All the ghosts were delighted to be spending another few days with the family, but Phoebe and Alex hadn't seen their dad looking so miserable for a long while. They were used to his bouts of sadness, how even when they were on holiday he would be worrying about something that might happen in the future, but this was different. For the past few days he'd hardly said a word. He didn't seem to want to look at them, spending all his time hidden away in his office. At mealtimes, all conversation about the ghosts was banned, and their mum kept shooting them warning glances whenever they strayed too close to the subject. As soon as their dad had finished eating, he would march straight back to his office and slam the door.

It was quite clear now that there would be no trip to Stonehenge, and nothing anyone could say would persuade him otherwise.

'What will happen to the ghosts?' Alex asked him

one morning, when he just couldn't help but bring the subject up.

'They don't belong with us,' his dad replied. 'They don't belong in the modern world. They will have to go back to where they came from.'

Fortunately, none of the ghosts were around to hear him.

'I've been thinking,' said Alex. Phoebe and Alex were in Alex's room, which for the moment was a ghost-free zone.

'I've been thinking about how the ghosts believe that they'll move on to a different stage of their afterlife. What if life after death is a bit like a computer game, where you have to complete one level before you can move on to the next? There could be lots of levels, and maybe heaven is the place you reach when you've completed them all?'

Phoebe rolled her eyes in despair.

'That's just plain ridiculous,' she said. 'You obviously spend far too much time staring into your computer screen. Let's worry about the problem here rather than making silly guesses.'

'It's not silly,' Alex said, but decided to let it drop all the same. 'What are we going to do then? Do you have any ideas?'

She thought for a moment, then said, 'I really don't know, but I can't bear the thought of them all going back to where they came from. It will feel like unfinished business, and after all, we promised we'd help them.'

'But how can we help them if dad keeps saying no? Do you think they could make their way to Stonehenge by themselves?'

'I doubt they'd have any idea where to go or which direction to go in. They need our help.'

'Could we take them ourselves?'

'Sure,' said Phoebe, 'and how are we going to do that? We're hardly likely to get permission to take a day trip to Stonehenge accompanied by ten ghosts.'

'Maybe we'll need to go without their permission,' Alex answered. 'We'll be in trouble, but at least we'll have done what we promised to do.'

'And how would we do that?'

'What if we pretend that we're going to school as usual one morning, but instead we take the ghosts to the station and go by train?'

'You mean play truant?' Phoebe sounded horrified. 'We'll be in double trouble. We'll be grounded by our parents and suffer days of detention at school.'

'But we'd have done the right thing. After all, a promise is a promise.'

'So *if* we do this, and I'm not saying yes, when would we go?'

'As soon as we can. We need to plan carefully first, but if we leave it too long, Dad will have told the ghosts to leave already. I can't believe he's being so mean to them.'

'You know what he's like. He's always got a lot on his plate. OK, let's think it through. I'll make a list.'

Alex smiled to himself. Another of Phoebe's famous lists. He remembered the one she'd made in the churchyard before they'd met Walter. One of his questions to ask a ghost had been, 'Can ghosts kiss?' Ned and Agnes had answered that one for him.

'Come on, pay attention, what will we need?'

By the time they'd finished the list looked like this:

Money for train tickets.
Mobile phone
Food to eat on the journey.
Maps
Information about Stonehenge
Change of underwear.

'Change of underwear?' Alex said. 'What on earth for?'

In case we need to stay overnight somewhere,' Phoebe said. 'Better safe than sorry.'

'What about the ghosts?' Alex asked. 'Will they need anything?'

Phoebe was about to start a second list, but after staring at the blank paper a while, she gave up. 'I suppose they've got by OK for the last three hundred years,' she said. 'They'll just need to make sure they stay with us and don't wander off somewhere.'

On Monday morning Alex and Phoebe returned to school after the half-term break. They'd argued all weekend about their plan for the ghosts. Alex, always far more impulsive than Phoebe, wanted to get going as soon as possible, but his sister held back. She had never deliberately missed school before, or lied to her parents about something as big as this.

Alex pointed out that they wouldn't be lying, just not saying where they were going, and that this was a subtle but important difference. They'd spent some time online the day before, Googling train times and ticket prices, and they'd found out that they needed to travel on two different trains.

That morning too, Rafe was his usual noisy self in the classroom.

'Mr Khan, can you get Alex and Phoebe to bring one of their ghosts into school so we can interview it?'

'Mr Khan, don't you want to see these ghosts? It's so unfair that they're keeping them hidden. Mr Khan—'

'Rafe, will you just be quiet. You're disturbing the whole class. I don't want to hear another word about ghosts.'

But for once Rafe had plenty who *did* want to hear him. Each break time he was surrounded, and his stories about the ghosts quickly became more and more exaggerated.

'Great big fangs, one of them had!' he said towards the end of lunch. 'And he was ten metres tall! He tried to scare me off, but I held my ground, and he ran off with his tail between his legs. That's why we couldn't get a picture of him.'

By the end of the day, Alex and Phoebe had made their decision. They would do what needed to be done, and they would do it the next day.

CHAPTER TWENTY-THREE

It seemed an ordinary sort of day. The sun was shining outside, and the weather looked set to be warm.

Phoebe and Alex got up at the usual time, washed (or in Alex's case, dragged a flannel across his face), went downstairs, ate breakfast, said their goodbyes, then left for school. They both had their backpacks containing their lunches and all the other items on Phoebe's list. They both had money too – it had been their eleventh birthdays a couple of weeks previously, and in all the excitement, neither of them had spent their gift money yet.

After that, the ordinary day began to turn into an extraordinary day.

Once out of the house, Phoebe and Alex quickly turned into the churchyard before they could be spotted by any of their friends. They walked past the graves and over to the back, where they stopped at the mausoleum with the tunnel entrance. They pushed open the iron gate and stepped inside. There they changed out of their school uniforms, bundled them up into a carrier bag, and left the bag out of sight in the tomb. Then they waited for twenty minutes till they were certain that anyone heading to school would have arrived, and then left the churchyard through a small gate at the back that led onto the street. Phoebe was still worried about what they were doing, and nothing Alex said seemed to reassure her.

The ghosts were already waiting for them, although it was difficult to make out their shapes as the sun was so bright. It had taken Phoebe and Alex some time the previous evening to convince them all to leave the luxury of the house and move on, but in the end everyone agreed it was the right thing to do. Phoebe had told them that at some point they would have to leave anyway, whether they liked it or not, because their dad's patience was running out. The idea of returning to the churchyard or to the drafty old castle wasn't an attractive one, so in the end they all agreed.

Now Walter was floating ahead of them as they walked the short distance to the station. The ghostly ladies started singing, and Ned floated close to Agnes, sneaking a quick kiss every now and then. Minnie kept complaining that they were going too fast for her and that they needed to remember her age.

They'd already decided that Phoebe should buy the train tickets, as she was taller than Alex and looked older. This went well, although tickets to Salisbury, the nearest railway station to Stonehenge, used up quite a lot of their money. They had to take the train to London first, and then catch another train to Salisbury from a different platform.

As the train came in, the ghosts pulled back. It was, of course, something else they had never experienced before.

'We need to be quick,' Alex said. 'When the doors open, everyone get on board.'

A couple of people boarding the train after them remarked that the air conditioning must have been stuck on extra strong. They quickly moved along the carriage, searching for a warmer spot.

Phoebe and Alex found seats and the ghosts arranged themselves around them.

'Not too close,' Alex told them. 'We don't want to feel like ice blocks by the time we get to London.'

Walter managed two lines of 'Highway to Hell' before they shushed him. Commuters stared around to see where the noise had come from, obviously not used to hearing AC/DC on their morning commute.

'All we need now,' Alex whispered to Phoebe, 'is for Walter to do one of his historical emanations, then we'll have the whole carriage to ourselves.'

Phoebe turned to him. 'Please, no. Not now.'

Walter pulled faces at a couple of small children in the adjacent seats, and their parents couldn't understand why they kept laughing and pointing. Then he floated up to the carriage roof and sat in the luggage rack dangling his legs.

'Stop showing off,' hissed Minnie. 'We don't want

to draw attention to ourselves.'

Ned stopped cuddling Agnes for a moment when a passenger with a large German Shepherd dog got on board. They saw a moment of fear on the dog's face as he either sensed or saw the ghosts, but as Ned came towards him, he wagged his tail and accepted a cold stroke.

Everything seemed to be going smoothly, and Alex and Phoebe were just starting to relax, when the connecting door to the carriage opened and Rafe sauntered in.

Phoebe and Alex looked at each other in horror. What on earth was he doing here? This was a disaster of the first magnitude.

'So you thought you'd leave me behind, did you?' Rafe said smugly. 'Thought you were so clever. But no one gets the better of me.'

'How did you find out?' Alex asked.

'I've been watching you. I knew you'd do something soon. I saw you leave this morning and turn into the churchyard. That's when I knew you were up to something. Clever, aren't I?'

'But you should be in school.'

'And so should you.'

Rafe sat down beside them as the ghosts moved away from him.

'What I don't know is where you're going. How about telling me that?'

'If we tell you, you'll be on the phone to your

photographer friend and letting him know. Then we'll have a gang of reporters waiting to meet us. That's not going to happen, Rafe.'

'Well, I'll just have to give you the pleasure of my company while I wait to find out then.'

Just then everyone heard a voice from the other end of the carriage. 'Tickets, please.'

Rafe looked worried. 'Or not... I haven't got a ticket. I'm going to have to hide in the toilet.'

He got up and hurried out of the carriage. Soon after the train pulled into a station and Alex did some quick thinking.

'Quick, everybody get off here. We'll wait for the next train.'

This they did, and in a few moments the doors had closed, and the train sped off.

'He's not so clever now,' said Alex.

'Nor are we,' said Phoebe looking around her. 'Walter's still on the train.'

CHAPTER TWENTY-FOUR

'Hello, is that Mrs Mitchell?'

'Yes, speaking.'

'This is Mr Khan, from Darvale School.'

'Oh, hello.'

'I'm just checking up on Phoebe and Alex, as they didn't arrive at school this morning. I know you usually contact us if they're absent.'

'Oh, gosh! They left for school same as usual. What's happened to them?'

'I don't know for certain, Mrs Mitchell, but I have my suspicions. One of their classmates, Rafe, is also absent.'

'It's not like them to do such a thing.'

'Mrs Mitchell, they have talked to me several times about *the* ghosts, and about their belief that they exist. Not only that, they told me that they'd *discovered ghosts in the churchyard* and that they needed to take them to Stonehenge.'

'You seem to know most of it, Mr Khan,' Mrs Mitchell said.

'I knew it. I knew they were real,' Mr Khan said.

There was a pause for a moment.

'I'm afraid I've been running something of a ghost hotel recently,' Mrs Mitchell confessed. 'My husband was supposed to take them to Stonehenge, but in the end he said no. He said the ghosts would have to go back to where they came from.'

'OK, I think perhaps you should contact your husband, Mrs Mitchell. I rather think they may have gone on the train. Maybe you could catch them before they get too far.'

'Thank you, I'll do that.'

She put down the phone then tried ringing Phoebe, but her phone was switched off. Alex's phone rang but she realised the ringing was coming from upstairs. He must have left his phone behind. It was another hour before Mrs Mitchell was able to reach her husband. He had been overseeing a funeral in a neighbouring village, and of necessity had his phone switched off. By the time she got through to him, Mrs Mitchell was very worried indeed.

When Rafe returned from the toilet after checking that the ticket inspector had moved on, he found that he'd been tricked. He hurried up and down the train to see if anyone was still on board and then returned to where they'd been sitting. As he wondered what to do next, he spotted something out of the corner of his eye...

*

Walter was actually quite frightened. Rafe was his last link to Phoebe and Alex. He knew they hated Rafe and wouldn't want him to have anything to do with him, but he had no idea what he'd do if he was left on his own. So he floated down in front of Rafe and made his presence known.

'They've abandoned you, Walter,' Rafe said.

'I wasn't watching. I wasn't quick enough!'

'Wasn't that how you ended up as a ghost in the first place?'

'I'm afraid so.'

'Where were you all going, Walter? Tell me that.'

Walter really didn't want to say. He tried frantically to think whether there was any way that he could avoid it, but he had no option. He needed to find the others again.

'We're going to a place called Stonehenge.'

'I've heard about that. They had human sacrifices there. Sounds like a fun place to me. Why were you going there?'

'Minnie thinks it's where we'll be able to stop being ghosts and move on to the next phase of our afterlife.'

Just then they heard the announcement that London would be their next stop and final destination. They were told to make sure they had all their belongings before they exited the train.

'You'd better stay with me, Walter,' Rafe said. 'London's a pretty big place. Your only chance of meeting the others again, and getting where you need to go, is to do everything I say.'

Alex and Phoebe only had to wait ten minutes before another train came along, but during that time Minnie moaned on and on and on about how useless Walter was.

'He was hopeless as a boy, got himself into all sorts of trouble, couldn't be relied upon to do anything right. And look at the way he got himself killed in that silly accident. All because he was playing a joke on Ned.'

'I'd give him a good thrashing if I could,' Ned said.

Meanwhile, the ghostly ladies seemed quite pleased to be rid of Walter. 'At least we won't have to hear that dreadful song anymore,' one of them said.

Phoebe and Alex, though, were extremely worried. They'd realised that Rafe was Walter's only hope of finding them again, and that Walter would have no choice but to lead Rafe straight to them.

'He won't have money for a ticket,' Phoebe said.

'He'll find a way to get on the train. The Rafes of this world always manage to get what they want, one way or another.'

When the London-bound train pulled into the station, everybody got on board, and in a short time they were arriving at Waterloo Station.

'Stay together,' warned Alex as they left the train. 'This will be incredibly crowded with people, and you won't want to get lost.'

They hurried along the platform in a cold huddle, two

children surrounded by a floating coalescence of ghosts.

At the ticket barrier, Phoebe and Alex showed their tickets and moved through into the station itself, the ghosts staying with them.

They stood in front of the huge display board showing the train destinations for the nineteen platforms at Waterloo Station. Eventually they found one that showed Salisbury and crossed the station concourse to reach it. They looked around for Rafe, but he wasn't visible. Where could he be? And more importantly, where was Walter?

The train was due to leave in five minutes, and Alex stood by the open door to the carriage, looking up and down the platform. At the last minute there was a commotion at the ticket barrier, and he saw Rafe leap the barrier and race along the platform. But was Walter with him?

The whistle was blown to signal the train's departure, and Alex saw Rafe spring down the platform, a couple of station officials huffing and puffing behind him. Alex watched as Rafe leapt aboard the train just as the doors were closing. The train started to move forward. Alex wondered if they might try to halt the train and remove Rafe but they didn't – both station officials were too busy wheezing and gasping for breath to raise the alarm.

The train was much fuller than the one they had been on earlier. Phoebe and Alex sat together on one seat while the ghosts all crowded together on the seat opposite them. People were still moving through the carriage, and a young woman saw what she thought were empty seats and sat down in one of them. She shivered, pulled a cardigan out of her bag and wrapped it tightly around her. When this did no good, she reached up for her coat from the rack above her head and put that on too. She looked round to see if there was a window open, then asked Alex and Phoebe if they felt cold. When they said they didn't, she collected her things, got up and went to find somewhere else to sit.

The ghosts seemed to have enjoyed the incident, and the ladies got up to have a walk along the carriage, and inspect what the other passengers were wearing. Phoebe and Alex could hear excited squeals every now and then, and saw passengers turn their heads, puzzled, trying to discover where the noises were coming from.

Their seat wasn't far from the buffet car, and people kept passing them with coffees. Ned enjoyed sniffing the aroma.

There was no sign of Rafe yet, and Phoebe and Alex were worried – not because they wanted to see Rafe (they never wanted to see Rafe), but because they still didn't know whether Walter was with him.

Just then a ticket collector entered their carriage, and their tickets were checked once more.

'Are you kids travelling alone?'

'Yes,' Phoebe answered. She'd prepared for this

sort of question. 'Our mother put us on the train in London and our aunt is meeting us at Salisbury.'

Phoebe hated lying, but felt that, right now, it was necessary. Besides, it was only a small lie compared to the much bigger lie that had enveloped them both today.

The ticket conductor smiled and left the carriage.

Shortly afterwards Rafe burst in.

'Well, hello, look who I've found. You thought you'd lost me, but you really weren't so clever after all.'

Phoebe decided to rise above this. 'Where's Walter?' she asked.

'I thought he was with you.'

'You know he isn't with us. He didn't get off the train when we did.'

Alex's eye was drawn to something moving in Rafe's pocket. A misty shape appeared and grew in size until they could all see Walter.

Walter looked really sorry for himself. In a sad voice he said, 'I'm really sorry for all the trouble I've caused.'

'No trouble as far as I'm concerned,' said Rafe. 'You gave me some much-needed information, and I didn't even have to threaten you for it. Now, what about something to eat? Anyone got any money?'

Phoebe and Alex took out their packed lunches and reluctantly shared them with Rafe, supposing it was the right thing to do.

'Wow, this is good quality stuff,' Rafe said, through mouthfuls of food. 'My mum's lunches aren't as tasty as these.'

From the seat opposite the ghosts looked on. How they longed to be able to enjoy food again. Ned and Agnes wanted to find the buffet car just so they could enjoy the smell of coffee being brewed, but Phoebe said they shouldn't separate. Besides, it was only ten minutes now until Salisbury.

She turned to Alex. 'I'm going to phone Mum now. She must be so worried and she needs to know where we are.'

It was a difficult conversation. Their mum was angry at first, then crying. Phoebe felt awful. Finally, she said she was happy that they'd made contact. They'd be driving down to meet them, she said. They were to wait at Stonehenge.

They all got off the train at Salisbury, making sure that Walter was with them this time. As they walked down the platform, Rafe's phone rang. It was his photographer friend, Dave. Rafe had previously given him the information that they were all bound for Stonehenge, and Dave was heading there too. *That's all we need*, Alex thought to himself. He watched Rafe smile as he hung up the phone; there would surely be money for providing the newspaper with such a photo opportunity.

The weather remained fine. With the sun out and the sky clear, everything was looking good for the right sort of Stonehenge sunset.

'We need to find the Stonehenge tour bus now,' Alex said. 'I hope it's not too expensive. We haven't got much money left.'

'I haven't got *any* money,' Rafe complained.

'Well, that's tough,' said Alex. 'I guess we'll see you back at school tomorrow.'

CHAPTER TWENTY-FIVE

Before they left, Alex had Googled how to get to Stonehenge. Now he knew that they were looking for a yellow and brown double decker bus that left every hour from Salisbury railway station.

They joined a queue waiting at a bus stop where the sign said 'Stonehenge Shuttle Bus'.

Phoebe and Alex had just enough money for bus tickets, but without money, Rafe was stuck. Sneaking onto a bus would be a much harder problem than a train. He pleaded with Phoebe to pay for him.

'Why on earth should I pay for you?' she said. 'All you've done so far is cause us problems. As far as I'm concerned you can stay here and work out how to find your own way home.'

'Ring home,' Alex advised him. 'Tell your parents where you are.'

Rafe walked off a short distance and pulled his phone out of his pocket.

The bus pulled in, and it looked as if every seat would be taken. The ghosts hovered in the aisle as passengers walked through them and shivered. There was nowhere else for them to go.

Resting his head against the window for a second, Alex was startled to see Ned and Agnes. They were still outside! They hadn't noticed their friends climbing onto the bus; they were too busy canoodling again. This was a word Alex had learnt from Minnie, an old-fashioned word that meant kissing and cuddling. Quickly he dashed off and reminded them why they'd come all this way. They joined the ladies in the aisle.

Suddenly the whole bus heard a loud and continuous farting noise as Walter shrank to the right size to perch on the seat between Alex and Phoebe. Alex heard the elderly gent behind him say, 'My, that was impressive!'

For a moment he was worried that the man had seen Walter transform, but he quickly realised that it was a comment on the noise. The man obviously thought that Alex was responsible.

Although he pleaded with the bus driver, Rafe finally had to accept that there was no way for him to board the bus. As it set off they watched him sitting on a bench looking very sorry for himself. Alex would have liked to have heard what Rafe's parents had to say when he had told them he was stranded in Salisbury. He didn't think they'd be very pleased with their son.

A few minutes later, a tour guide at the front of the bus began a commentary:

'Good afternoon, ladies and gentlemen, it is my

pleasure to tell you some facts about Stonehenge while we travel there. Nobody knows for certain why Stonehenge was built on Salisbury Plain, or even what it was built for. We estimate that it has stood for between four thousand and five thousand years. Some of the stones, called bluestones, were transported here from a quarry in Wales, many miles away. Many of the stones have names. There's a heel stone, an altar stone and another called the slaughter stone. I dread to think what happened there...'

The guide paused. She could hear faint singing. Phoebe and Alex could hear it too, and so, it seemed, could the rest of the passengers. The guide was used to people listening to her. Nobody before had ever interrupted her commentary in this way.

Everybody was looking around, trying to spot who might be so rude as to sing in the middle of their tour. Only Phoebe and Alex knew that it was their invisible friends, the ladies from Northmead Castle, singing as they swayed about in the aisle. They recognised the tune too. It was one of their music teacher's favourite songs, a song that King Henry VIII had enjoyed listening to over five hundred years before.

'Greensleeves was my delight,
Greensleeves my heart of gold.
Greensleeves was my heart of joy,
And who but my lady Greensleeves...'

The volume rose and the singing grew sweeter as the ladies became more enthusiastic, and soon several of the passengers were joining in too. The tour guide sat down in her seat, totally mystified. There wasn't any way that she could talk above the singing, so she abandoned her plans and took out her phone.

The ghostly ladies reached the end of their song and stopped singing. It was quiet for a moment till suddenly...

'We're on the highway to hell, we're on the highway to hell...'

'Shut up, Walter,' Alex hissed.

After it had been quiet for a few minutes, the tour guide stood up again and started giving out more information. She finished with a warning.

'In 1971, a group of young people were camping close to the stones. There was a bad storm in the night and screams were heard coming from the area. A policeman nearby reported seeing a blue light. By the time the policeman had reached the campsite there was nobody to be seen, just a few tent pegs and the ashes of a campfire. So, please be warned, strange things happen at Stonehenge...'

Alex and Phoebe looked at each other. Could that be the portal that Minnie had told them about?

CHAPTER TWENTY-SIX

When the bus stopped, the ghosts were reluctant to get out, hesitant about the prospect of taking that next step into the unknown.

The driver was impatient for Phoebe and Alex to leave so that he could usher in passengers waiting to board for their trip back to Salisbury. Finally, they managed to persuade everyone, but a cold feeling awaited the new passengers as they moved through the ghosts who were coming down the steps.

The car park at Stonehenge was busy, with lots of coaches bringing tourists speaking all sorts of languages as they passed by.

Phoebe and Alex could see the visitors' centre that they had read about in their research online. They suddenly felt hungry.

'How much money have we got?' Alex asked Phoebe.

'Not much, but I did find a bit extra when I was looking in my bag on the bus. Mum gave me a five pound note the other day when I went shopping. I didn't spend it and forgot to give it back.'

'That's great,' said Alex. 'Perhaps they sell doughnuts.'

'Excuse me,' said Minnie politely. 'What are we to do while you're at the food place?'

'I think we should go in with them,' said Ned. 'One of the small pleasures afforded to a ghost is at least being able to smell food and remember what it was like. I say we all go in for a good sniff around.'

Inside the café there was a mixture of smells – coffee, bacon and sweet sugary smells that attracted Walter straight away. Four people were sitting down to a late lunch, and they were quickly surrounded by Ned, Agnes and the ghostly ladies.

Phoebe and Alex could see Ned with his nose approaching a half-eaten burger, taking a huge sniff. He wore an expression of delight on what they could see of his face. They heard one of the diners say that she didn't feel very hungry anymore, and that she really needed to go and find somewhere warm. The others agreed and all four left their food and moved away.

The ghosts all carried on sniffing the food, which proved to be great entertainment for a giggling toddler at the next table. His parents were amused by their son's laughter, although they had no idea what had caused it.

Phoebe and Alex paid for a drink each and a slice of chocolate cake, which they shared between them.

'You'd better enjoy this, Alex, because that has used

up all of our money.'

Ned was looking longingly at the cake, and Phoebe felt so sorry for him.

Walter floated around the room, much to the delight of several small children who watched him pass by.

Minnie set herself up as spokesperson for the ghosts.

'Before we travel on to the next stage of the afterlife – if we are able to, that is – I think we should all thank Alex and Phoebe for all the help they have given us.'

'Yes, we should. Thank you, thank you, thank you!' said all the ghostly ladies as one.

'Well, we really wish you could stay with us,' Phoebe said. 'It's been such fun.'

'In some ways we'd like to stay,' said Minnie. 'We were very comfortable living with your family, but really we've outlived our welcome. The party's over for us, and we're like the last guests to realise it's time to leave. There's nothing here for us, we can't do anything meaningful, all we can do is watch and wait and wonder at what we see around us.'

'I agree,' said Agnes, who had been listening to Minnie. 'We've seen the modern world and all its wonders, but we've also watched the news on television, and in many ways the world hasn't changed much in three hundred years. There are still wars being fought, there are still people being violent towards each other. It's time we moved on.'

'If we stay,' said Ned, 'sooner or later there'll be

some ghosthunter who finds a way to track us down, to restrain us in some way, and then we'll be exhibited as freaks. We don't want that.'

However, I do know this,' Ned continued, turning to Phoebe and Alex, 'I'm a better man, or should I say a better ghost, for having met you two and seeing how determined you've been to help us. I can't thank you enough.'

Everyone sat in silence for a moment till Walter called out, 'Where is this circle of stones though? We're here, but we haven't seen it yet.'

Alex was wondering about that too. There was no sign of it from the car park, and it wasn't visible from the café either.

They went back outside and looked all around them.

'Where do we go?' Ned asked. 'Do you know, Minnie?'

'I don't. It's all so different to when I came here as a girl. As far as I can remember we came in a horse and cart and wandered around among the stones. We annoyed our dad by playing chase around the stones and climbing all over them.'

Their food finished, Phoebe and Alex led the ghosts out into the courtyard and looked around. They noticed that everyone seemed to be gathering in one place, perhaps waiting for transport of some kind to take them to the stone circle. They saw a sign that said Shuttle Bus, and as they watched, something the length of a short train crawled into view and stopped right by them. The passengers stepped down, chattering about how amazing it was to see the ancient stones.

'Looks like that's the way to go,' Phoebe said, 'but they won't let us on without tickets.'

Phoebe and Alex looked at each other, their hearts sinking. They hadn't counted on there being a charge to see the stones. They didn't have any money left for tickets. They'd thought it would be like a museum, where you could go in for free and learn everything you wanted.

'It's OK for you,' Alex said to the ghosts, 'you can pass through fences and float to wherever it is, but we can't. We'll have to say goodbye here and hope you find your way.'

That wasn't what Alex had wanted at all. He wanted to see what happened when the ghosts passed through the portal. Surely they hadn't made all this effort just to lose them now?

Someone called out that the next bus would be the final one of the day. It was looking like the ghosts would have to set off on their own.

At that moment Phoebe's phone rang. Mrs Mitchell said that they were about an hour away and that they would see them in the car park on arrival. Alex looked at Phoebe. Could they get to the stones and be back to meet them in time?

From where they were standing, they could see a line of visitors walking across the fields.

'I wonder,' Phoebe said, 'if that is also a route to the stones.'

They all got up and moved to take a closer look. There was a gate that an official from Stonehenge was opening to let people through. Beyond that gate was a second gate, which no one was checking.

As they watched, the walkie-talkie that the official wore on his belt beeped and crackled. He turned aside to answer it, and Alex sprung forward, hissing at Phoebe to follow. They both ran as quickly as they could along the path. The ghosts were following too, and over their shoulders they could hear Minnie complaining that she couldn't keep up with everyone.

No one seemed to be bothered about them, so as they approached the second gate, Phoebe and Alex slowed to a walking pace. To the right of them was a grass-covered mound, and as they passed by, the stone circle came into view. Everyone stopped to stare.

'Oh my!' said Minnie.

'Wow!' Walter exclaimed.

'Oh, Ned!' whispered Agnes.

Then they heard the noise of a car approaching along the path, and an official-looking vehicle came to a stop alongside them. A uniformed man with 'English Heritage' printed on his jacket got out of the car.

'We're closing soon,' he said, 'you will need to get back to the centre quite quickly.'

Phoebe and Alex looked at each other in dismay. They needed time to say goodbye before they left their ghostly friends. Friends was how they saw them now – very strange friends, otherworldly friends, but friends nevertheless.

Phoebe thought quickly, then spoke quickly too. 'Our parents won't be here to pick us up for another half hour. They dropped us off to look around for a history project that we're doing at school. We have a grandmother who is always telling us about how she could walk around the stones as a girl, how she could touch them and wonder at their magic.'

Alex took a moment to realise that his sister wasn't talking about their own grandmother. She was talking about Minnie, who had become something of a ghostly grandmother.

The thing about Phoebe was that no one could ever believe that she wasn't telling the truth. Her face was so open and honest, even when she was lying.

'Yes, it used to be possible to touch the stones,' said the man, 'but there was a lot of damage. People used to carve their names on them. We still check them every day. That's where I'm heading now.'

'Oh wow! Could we come with you?'

'And your names are?'

'Phoebe and Alex.'

'Well, Phoebe and Alex, I'm Jack, and I would be happy to show you the stones, but I don't want your parents arriving at the visitors' centre and not knowing where you are.'

'I can phone them,' Phoebe said. 'You could speak

to them.'

At lightning speed, she had her phone out and was calling their parents. She passed the phone to Jack.

Very quickly Jack told their parents who he was and what he planned to do. He said he'd have them back at the centre soon after Mr and Mrs Mitchell arrived. They didn't know when that would be, he reported after he'd hung up, as their car was stuck in a traffic queue.

Jack led Phoebe and Alex to a gate in the fence, which he unlocked, and then led them through. Their ghostly friends were already through the fence and drifting towards the stone circle.

As the gate was being locked behind them, they all heard a shout.

'Oh no!' said Alex.

Running towards them along the path were Rafe and Dave.

'I wish I had my rolling pin,' they heard Ned mutter.

CHAPTER TWENTY-SEVEN

'Bet you thought you'd got rid of me!' Rafe yelled at them as he came to a halt. He was panting, out of breath from running, but Dave was far worse. He was wheezing badly and holding on to a fence post to keep himself upright. It was obvious that he wouldn't be able to say anything until he'd caught his breath.

'Dave, Dave, take photographs!' Rafe implored. 'We must have evidence.'

All the ghosts turned their backs on Rafe; they had no intention of posing for the camera. Dave, however, was finding it hard to focus his camera while gasping for air.

'Dave,' yelled Rafe again, 'they're getting away, stop them!'

'Who's getting away?' said Jack, 'and who are you?'

Alex and Phoebe started running, getting ever closer to the stones. Rafe was running alongside the fence, waving his phone around in the hope that he'd capture something on film.

'Look,' Rafe yelled, 'can't you see all these ghosts?'

Rafe's words were tumbling over themselves as

they did when he got excited. Phoebe and Alex were used to this. They'd seen it happen a million times, most recently when he'd struggled to convince Mr Khan about the existence of ghosts. He talked fast and made very little sense.

'They're all trying to get to the stones so they can find the portal and move on to the next stage of their afterlife! We have to stop them! We need photos, evidence! Don't let them go!'

Eventually his words trailed away. Even he could see the impossibility of getting Jack to see what he was seeing. Anyway, there was nothing anyone could do. Even if Jack had tried, he'd have had no way of stopping them. You can't hold on to ghosts, or bundle them into a car and expect them to stay there. They were mist, and like mist they drifted wherever they wanted to go.

Rafe screamed in frustration, and his scream echoed around the landscape.

'What on earth is this all about?' said Jack, looking flustered. 'What do you mean ghosts? I can't see anything.'

As Phoebe and Alex approached the stones, the ghosts were visible, outlined against a red-tinted sky.

'Walter,' called Alex. 'I think you should all show yourselves to Jack. He needs to know why we're here.'

Jack's mouth fell open as one by one the ghosts grew visible. Ned and Agnes were holding each other tightly and Minnie had sat herself down on one of the stones. The ghostly ladies were arranged in a line while Walter was floating up to perch on one of the horizontal stones supported by two vertical ones.

Dave hastily tried to snap some photos, but the ghosts noticed and quickly faded again.

'I can't believe what I've just seen,' said Jack. 'I've worked here for twenty years, and I've never come across anything like that.'

He took out his phone and called a work colleague, telling him that there were two people on the pathway who needed to be removed. Then he told him to bring the high-res camera, as there was something important to the history of Stonehenge that needed recording.

As he finished his call, the cloud cover began to break and a ray of sun shone down on them.

'Do you think there'll be a proper sunset tonight?' Phoebe asked.

'I think there could be,' said Jack. 'I've seen this happen many times. It's a mix of sun and cloud all day, and then suddenly the clouds melt away to leave a brilliant sunset, but I don't think it will happen for half an hour or so, if it happens at all.'

'And do you think one of these archways could be a type of portal?'

'Well, they have been called "the Gateway to the Gods", and Stonehenge is positioned where fourteen ley lines intersect.'

'What are ley lines?'

'They're invisible lines of energy, and some people

like to believe that they criss-cross the earth. The points where they meet have long been considered powerful, even magical places.'

The ghosts had all gathered around Jack, and he shivered as he felt the coldness they brought with them. The crack in the clouds was widening and a pattern of shadows and light was spreading across the surrounding fields.

'This must be the place!' said Minnie excitedly. 'We've waited so long for this, so many dark and dreary years…'

'Maybe we'll be a choir of angels when we get there,' said the green lady, to a chorus of approval from the other castle ladies.

'Oh yes.'

'I'd love that.'

'It's the singing that kept us going.'

'Maybe we can sing in a blaze of light. It will be so different from singing just to get through the darkness.'

Jack was conscious of voices all around him and was desperately trying to work out where they were coming from.

As they watched the sunset grew wider.

'One of the strange facts about this place,' said Jack, 'is that it has amazing acoustics. Sound reverberates similarly to the way it does in a cathedral or a modern concert hall.'

Alex looked at Phoebe. Where was Walter? A few moments later they got their answer.

'WE'RE ON THE HIGHWAY TO HELL,
WE'RE ON THE HIGHWAY TO HELL!'

Hearing what Jack had just said had been too much of a temptation for Walter. He just had to test it out.

'If I have to spend eternity listening to that racket, then I'd rather stay here,' complained Minnie. 'At least it was quiet in the churchyard.'

'They used to hold festivals here in the sixties and seventies,' said Jack, 'but nothing like that volume has rung out around these hills since then. I'm impressed.'

Walter floated across to bask in Jack's praise.

'I've been practicing,' he said, suddenly visible and glowing with pride. 'Do you like AC/DC?'

Jack smiled. 'Of all the questions I might have thought a ghost would ask me, if I ever met one, that's one that would never have crossed my mind.'

'Dreadful noise,' moaned Minnie. 'I don't want him anywhere near me in the next life. I'm sure he'll be kicked out of wherever we're going if he comes out with that too often.'

Ned looked at Alex and Phoebe. 'I'll never thank you enough for helping me find Agnes again.'

'Yes, you are both very special people,' said Agnes.

'And I can't thank you enough for definitively answering one of my questions about ghosts,' said Alex. 'Now I know for sure that ghosts can kiss each other... although I'll need to do further research as to whether two ghosts carrying their heads can kiss.'

Ned chuckled. 'Hissed kisses are OK, but nothing

like the real thing. If only I had one more chance to kiss Agnes like we did when we were alive. You're too young to understand, Alex, but one day you will, and you'll remember what I said.'

Everyone stayed silent for a while, the humans with their backs to the stones, the ghosts drifting around the circle, until Minnie whispered, 'I'm worried. Everyone's looking to me for guidance. They're asking where we should stand and when. I'm not sure what to tell them.' She looked at Jack. 'Where would you think we need to be?'

'I don't know,' Jack replied. 'But if I were to take a guess, I'd say the middle archway of the triple set of arches. That's where the rays of the sun touch when it's sinking.'

'How much longer do we have to wait?' Alex asked.

'Not very long at all now, by my reckoning, just a matter of minutes.'

Minnie collected the ghosts together and got everyone to stand in the archway that Jack had suggested. The castle ladies were singing again, a soft, sad song. *A lament*, Phoebe thought to herself. She'd recently learnt that word and was pleased to be able to make use of it.

At that moment they heard noises from the footpath. Jack's colleague had arrived with his high-res camera, and with him were Alex and Phoebe's parents. Rafe, ever the opportunist, was trying to slip through the gate too.

Dave, meanwhile, had actually tied himself to the fence with his belt buckle, and was refusing to budge. He hoped that he was in position to scoop the most amazing photograph of his career.

Rafe, at his second attempt, barged everyone aside and managed to get through. He was now running towards the stones, zig-zagging as he went to give Jack the slip.

By the time he reached the circle, though, Jack was ready and managed to bring him down with a splendid rugby tackle.

Rafe was shouting and protesting vigorously, 'You can't do that to me!'

'I think you'll find that I can. I am authorised to restrain anyone who illegally enters Stonehenge.'

'Just shut up for once, Rafe,' said Phoebe. 'Keep quiet and watch. This could be magic.'

And amazingly Rafe did just that.

Mr and Mrs Mitchell moved to stand with Phoebe and Alex. 'We're so glad you're safe,' their dad said.

Rays from the dying sun were now creeping through the edge of the circle, and the sky was beginning to exhibit a stunning mix of red, orange, yellow and purple hues.

It was surely set to be a sunset fit for a king, and the grandest of welcomes to those lost ones who had missed their chances the first time around.

As everyone watched they saw the misty outlines of Minnie, Ned, Agnes, and the castle ladies, all silhouetted against the sunset. But there were other figures too, more ghostly outlines taking shape, a gathering of ghosts drifting into the circle from the surrounding fields.

There were ladies in long flowing dresses, soldiers in uniform, farm labourers, children too. There was a headless ghost being led by others, a procession of figures trailing each other towards the centre archway. Some were stumbling, falling, picking themselves up again; others were floating above the ground. Small children were running, playing tag.

The rays of the sun shone on their faces. Some were fearful, nervously looking around themselves; some held their hands together in prayer. Others were looking up at the skies, wonder in their faces.

They moved on, reaching the stones before pausing, looking around for the last time and taking that final step beneath the archway. There they vanished, leaving only dust to float in the air.

Jack gasped. 'I have never seen anything like this. It makes me wonder if the ancients knew something we don't. Is Stonehenge a waiting room, is it really an exit from this world to another?'

They continued watching as the Northmead Castle ladies seemed to dance towards the archway before disappearing one by one. Then Minnie moved forward, paused, looked round, gave a wave and then vanished like the rest. Ned and Agnes were the only figures remaining now, and seemed reluctant to move forward. But then arm in arm, heads high, faces raised, they stepped into the archway.

'Where's Walter?' Phoebe said. 'We must have missed him.'

'Perhaps he ran through with the other children,' Alex said. 'He would have liked that.'

'I wish we could have seen him go.'

Just one remaining flicker of sunlight lingered on the stones, and then it was over.

Or so they thought.

Rafe leapt to his feet, and at lightning speed he dashed towards the archway. Jack tried to catch him, but it was no use. As he reached the arches, there was a flash of light that spotlit the stones before mist enveloped everything. Nothing could be seen for a minute or two until the mist evaporated, but when it finally cleared, the sun had disappeared, and it looked like Rafe had gone with the ghosts.

CHAPTER TWENTY-EIGHT

Phoebe was distraught.

'What can we do?' she cried.

Alex couldn't believe it either. He didn't like Rafe, and he'd caused them lots of trouble, but Alex didn't wish him harm.

'What can we do?' Phoebe repeated.

Jack was searching around the stones as if Rafe might be hiding somewhere, but before anyone could decide on any sort of plan, Rafe was back again.

One second he wasn't there, the next second he was: dazed, shaken and obviously very frightened.

It seemed like whatever had taken the ghosts had rejected Rafe.

Alex wasn't surprised. Nobody would want a pain in the bum like Rafe, not even some supernatural force.

Jack was asking him if he felt all right. He looked Rafe over, tested his arms and his legs, pulled him to his feet and concluded that, apart from shock, the boy seemed fine.

'What happened?' he asked Rafe.

Rafe was looking around, still dazed, and when he

answered, his voice sounded shaky too.

'I saw a light, an incredibly bright light. There were figures in the distance, shadowy figures, coming towards me. I think they may have been aliens. Do you think they experimented on me? I've heard about strange happenings like that. Maybe they've changed me…'

'Hopefully for the better,' Alex whispered to Phoebe.

'But what about the ghosts?' asked Phoebe. 'Did you see what happened to them? Where did they go?'

Rafe shook his head. There were no answers to be had from him, but Phoebe hoped that wherever they'd gone, it was where they'd needed to be.

Phoebe and Alex's parents wanted answers too.

'We've no idea what we've just seen,' Mrs Mitchell said, 'but William Shakespeare wrote in one of his plays, I think it was *Hamlet*, about there being more things in heaven and earth than we can ever dream of. That's not the exact quote, but it's something like that.'

'More importantly though,' their dad said, 'how did you manage to make this trip on your own?'

They tried to explain but it wasn't sounding at all convincing. Then their dad said, 'Well you did the right thing, and I'm proud of you both, but it was the wrong way to do it.'

'But how else could we have done it, Dad? You wouldn't take us.'

'I made the wrong decision,' he said, 'and I'm sorry. We're just glad that you're both safe. Your mum and I did a lot of talking on the drive down, and we'll tell you about what we've decided while we drive home. But now we need to set off. It will be way past midnight by the time we get back.'

Jack said how delighted he was to have met Phoebe and Alex.

'My eyes have been opened,' he said. 'I'm just gobsmacked by what just happened. I'm not sure whether there are any answers to be found, but I need to look for them regardless. It seems that my friend took some amazing photos on his camera, and these will need to be investigated by scientists and photography experts.'

The only person who seemed unhappy was Dave. Despite taking as many photos as he could, he hadn't been close enough to get the best results. He pleaded with Jack to let him have copies of the the pictures his friend had taken, but Jack told him that they were private property.

Back at the car park, as darkness descended, everyone heard raised voices. Rafe was arguing with Dave, then pleading with him, but to no avail.

'How am I supposed to get home?' they heard him whine.

'That's your problem, Rafe,' Dave said. 'I'm not in charge of you. I'm going straight back to London.'

'But what do I do? I'll be stuck here. And it's dark!'

'Phone your parents. They'll need to sort you out. You're not my responsibility.'

And with that Dave got into his car, slammed the door, and drove away.

'Mr Mitchell,' Rafe called out, 'can I come home with you?'

'Give me one good reason why I should take you home, Rafe. All you've done is give me headaches for the past fortnight.'

'But I haven't got anywhere to go! I don't have any money, and I can't stay here.'

'You certainly can't,' said Jack. 'We're closed for the night now.'

'Have you told your parents where you are?'

'Yes, but they won't come and get me. They say I'll have to phone the police.'

Mr Mitchell knew Rafe's parents and wasn't at all surprised by their attitude. Their son was always in trouble for one thing or another, and today Rafe had obviously caused them a great deal of stress. Rafe's father was probably hoping that the police would stick him in a cell for the night. Maybe that would teach him a lesson.

'Get in the back, Rafe.'

'Oh, thank you, Mr Mitchell!'

Phoebe and Alex looked at each other. The prospect of travelling with Rafe was not appealing at all.

After they had been driving for a few miles, during which Rafe had said nothing, he suddenly said, 'Could I ask you a question please, Mr Mitchell?'

'Go on.'

'When I do my work experience at secondary school, could I come and work for you in the funeral parlour?'

'Why's that, Rafe?'

'I'd get the chance to open a coffin lid.'

Alex groaned. Phoebe looked furious.

'Yes, Rafe, of course you can.'

Phoebe looked at Alex in amazement.

Rafe fist pumped the air. 'Yes!'

'You can open a coffin lid, Rafe, but it will be an empty one. I'd hoped that what you've been through today at the stones might have knocked some sense into you, but no such luck. You don't show enough respect for the dead, Rafe. You want to treat them as circus freaks, something to be gawped at. You really need to do some growing up. Find yourself some more suitable interests.'

Rafe grumbled but said nothing, and a few minutes later he took out his phone and started scrolling through his photographs. Most were blurry and could have been anything, but there were one or two that were clearer. He showed them to Alex and Phoebe. 'At least I have my evidence still.'

They travelled on until the lights of a motorway service centre could be seen up ahead.

'I'm not driving any further,' said Mr Mitchell, 'without getting something to eat and a coffee to keep me awake. Is anyone else hungry?'

Everyone else *was* hungry. Rafe was also desperate for the toilet, and after they'd parked the car, he left in great haste, heading towards the entrance.

Their dad turned around to face them.

'I repeat, what you two did today was wonderful. You took a risk, but you planned it well and achieved the result that you wanted. You caused us some worry and stress while you were doing it, but we're proud of you. I've never been a risk taker, never taken chances, and our lives have closed down because of it. I've spent too long worrying, and causing your mum worry too. That's going to change from now.

'I work with the dead. Black clothes and a sad expression are part of the job. I've decided now that I'm going to have an on/off switch. When I leave work I'll press the switch and leave it all behind. I need to do more, get out more – we all do. I may be an undertaker, but I can still enjoy rock 'n' roll. It's time to dust off my old albums and get my guitar down from the loft. Maybe we'll all go to the Glastonbury Festival next year. What do you think?'

Alex and Phoebe didn't know what to think, but their dad was smiling and their mum was smiling too. That was good enough for now.

'Now, let's go and get some food and some hot drinks.'

Alex nudged Phoebe and pointed. In Rafe's hurry to get out of the car he had left his phone on the back seat.

Phoebe grabbed it. 'Shall I steal this, or throw it in the nearest bin?'

'You could do either, but I suppose it doesn't matter now. The ghosts are gone. No one can try to capture them, or make a study of them, they don't exist anymore.'

Phoebe dropped the phone back on the seat. 'You're right. Let Rafe say what he wants. Everyone will get bored of him sooner or later.'

Their dad locked the car, and as they walked towards the building, Alex turned to Phoebe.

'I really wish I'd seen Walter when all the other ghosts suddenly appeared. I still feel that we didn't get to say a proper goodbye. I'll really miss him. He became a strange sort of friend over the time he was with us. It didn't seem to matter that he was of another time, he was still a kid.'

'Yes, he told me once how he would have liked to have grown up.'

'When you think about it, he's been a child, both human and ghost, for over three hundred years.'

'And he wasn't sure about where he was going after Stonehenge. He thought that maybe it would be a place for older ghosts. I do hope he'll be happy there.'

Back in the car there were sandwiches and chips for everyone. Mrs Mitchell had picked up lots of sachets of tomato sauce too, knowing how much Alex liked to spread it over his chips.

Everyone sat quietly eating.

'What we need,' said Mr Mitchell, 'is some music to keep us awake, or rather to keep me awake on the drive home. I just need to find the right playlist.'

Suddenly the car was filled with the sound of a familiar riff.

'Only one band is suitable for the occasion, I think, even if your mum doesn't like them…'

'Oh, please don't play that song,' Mrs Mitchell protested.

'I think we should hear it once more and celebrate the wonderful thing that Phoebe and Alex achieved today.'

'*I'm on the highway to hell…*'

It was AC/DC's greatest hit, and their dad joined in with gusto. He still knew most of the words from his teenage years. He started playing air guitar too, which wasn't easy in the confined space of the car.

Phoebe and Alex weren't used to seeing him so happy.

Eventually, at their mum's insistence, their dad stopped singing. Then, faintly, very faintly, they could hear another voice, a whisper of a voice at first, but gradually getting louder. It was a crackle of a voice, both young and old at the same time, and then suddenly the singing stopped.

Alex felt a slight movement in his pocket, a familiar wriggle as if something was trying to get comfortable. Then there was a cough.

'I'm awfully sorry. I got scared when all the other ghosts came crowding in, and I missed my chance again. Can I please come home with you?'

'Oh, Walter!'